ONCE UPON A TIME IN

'The funniest and most magnetic love story for decades'

Based on a true story

Written by DBJ Swarbrick

Order this book online at www.trafford.com/08-0014
or email orders@trafford.com

Most Trafford titles are also available at major online book retailers.

Note for Librarians: A cataloguing record for this book is available from Library and Archives Canada at www.collectionscanada.ca/amicus/index-e.html

ISBN: 978-1-4251-6805-6

We at Trafford believe that it is the responsibility of us all, as both individuals and corporations, to make choices that are environmentally and socially sound. You, in turn, are supporting this responsible conduct each time you purchase a Trafford book, or make use of our publishing services. To find out how you are helping, please visit www.trafford.com/responsiblepublishing.html

Our mission is to efficiently provide the world's finest, most comprehensive book publishing service, enabling every author to experience success. To find out how to publish your book, your way, and have it available worldwide, visit us online at www.trafford.com/10510

www.trafford.com

North America & international
toll-free: 1 888 232 4444 (USA & Canada)
phone: 250 383 6864 ♦ fax: 250 383 6804 ♦ email: info@trafford.com

The United Kingdom & Europe
phone: +44 (0)1865 722 113 ♦ local rate: 0845 230 9601
facsimile: +44 (0)1865 722 868 ♦ email: info.uk@trafford.com

10 9 8 7 6 5 4 3 2 1

Acknowledgements

I would like to thank my dearest wife Yecora for all her help, love and inspiration to enable me to create this book. I would also like to thank the people of Mexico for their huge generosity and amazing outlook on life and love to which I am forever indebted, not to mention all my Mexican family for their hospitality and understanding.

I would also like to thank my amazing parents, brothers and sisters who have provided me with the best upbringing packed with fun and laughter, more than anyone could ever have wished for. I am also much indebted to my life time friends who must have written half this book themselves without even knowing.

Once upon a time in La Boom is based on a true love story, some names and places have been changed for privacy and story telling purposes.

Introduction

What is more important, to have your own transport to get you to work or to sell your car for funds and make sure you join your friends on the next summer holiday?

My view is normally to take the safe option and make sure that first and foremost that you make it to work on time and earn the money to pay for things later. That is not the order an optimist would take and being a huge optimist I decided to take the bull by the horns, throw caution to the wind and not miss the second consecutive holiday. After all what is public transport there for, to be used of course and contrary to James Bond you only live once.

The previous summer holiday had consisted of twelve of the old school gang touring through the US with their golf clubs having the time of their lives. I unfortunately didn't make that trip. I hadn't missed many road trips over the years but owing to some well needed spinal repair work and subsequent dismal sick pay I had to concede but I wasn't going to miss this year's trip. It was the new Millennium and I had eight months previously become single again so I certainly wasn't going to miss out again, no way. After all it was a case of no regrets and I was to follow in the footsteps of my friend who broke his neck when he was nine, he hasn't looked back since!

This years holiday was being arranged for eight of the gang and the idea was to try something fresh, somewhere no one had ever been so what better place to go than Mexico? The travel agent assured us that there was something there for everyone, how true did that turn out to be?......

Chapters

Chapter 1

Tickets, passport, money….?

Time was pressing on and Baz was rapidly organising the summer holiday which was to be better than all the rest. He wanted me to make up my mind if I was going or not, I was sure he wanted me to go because I could tell he didn't want to me to regret missing out like last year.

Last year's golf trip to the US was legendary, apparently and the stories that came from it were more than enough to provide an incentive to join the gang this year. The guys even had T-shirts printed with the classy Ralph Lauren Polo emblem showing the Polo player on horse back, however the text was less than classy which read "Tonight we drink, tommorrow we ride, complete with miss-spelling.

I hadn't had the best start to the year two thousand, I couldn't seem to get on top with my money situation and I had a difficult break up and I was now living alone on a single income. I assured Baz that I would definitely be going this time and to include me on his list, now to find the money! The situation was grim; I was living in Preston, commuting to Manchester every day for work which usually took an hour and a half each way during rush hour. So I needed a plan to 'free up' some money. The only way really was to sell my car, I was living on my monthly wages but running out of cash after the second week of every month, then I would borrow three hundred pounds from my sister, my dad or a friend, then pay it all back once I'd been paid then go through the same routine from month to month. Although I had a good job I was basically living like a student and owing to my new single life I was also partying like one too. No real harm in that I thought, at Twenty nine years of age, with my own house, a good job and more close friends than anyone could imagine. In fact my house became a meeting point for most social and sporting events, so no real complaints other than the need for a cash injection.

It had dawned on me that if I sell the car then I will have to get out of bed much earlier to catch a bus, then walk to the train station from the bus stop, travel on the busiest train you've ever seen [with two carriages, I've never understood that, why only two carriages, one of life's mysteries I suppose] then hop off the train to set upon my second bus journey of the morning just before I embark on my second and longest walk of the morning, all to be at my desk before eight am for some number crunching. A piece of cake, no problem at all, I wished! It would actually be costing more money than if I had the car, "oh what the hell just sell it" I thought something will always turn up. Maybe my boss will finally get me a company vehicle after all my previous attempts. Maybe I could get a lift off a friend, maybe I'll win the lottery or maybe it will be the worst move I've ever made.

It took a little time before I managed to convince my parents that I was in control of the situation and that I fully knew what I was doing. I had already paid a visit to the bank of Dad a couple of years previously and hadn't finished paying that loan so there was no way I could ask if they could bail me out just to go on holiday, I was about to enter into unknown waters but optimistically I felt that I couldn't lose, I somehow felt strangely positive about the whole idea.

It was only four weeks until the holiday to Cancun, Mexico and I needed to pay my flight and hotel which was one thousand pounds the following week to secure the deal. The following morning I arrived at work for the last time in my battered old Ford Fiesta, I had only bought the car eight months previously for the simple reasons that it was cheap to maintain and very cheap on gas, either way it had to go this weekend. My work colleagues looked on and sniggered nervously, I think they even knew I was taking a big gamble, my boss's opinion was that of silence, maybe he knew something I didn't, maybe my shiny new company car was being fitted with go fast stripes as we didn't speak?

It was Saturday morning and following some previous ground work I arrived bright and early at the garage that I felt sure would exchange the exact amount of cash needed for the trip of a lifetime. I sat in the grubby waiting room for my turn to come and pictured the build up to the summer holiday; I was also looking forward to tomorrow being Sunday which was possibly the best day of the week for a singleton like me. We would usually have a few drinks the night before then have a well deserved sleep in until lunch time then it would be time for a full day of eating, watching sport and boozing, we were living the dream but although we hadn't realised it our clocks were ticking. In other words we weren't getting any younger and there would come a time when we would have to grow up and make decisions.

So my turn came at the garage and the guy led me outside to look at the pile of crap I was hoping would finally prove its worth. He looked around the car, scratched his chin and didn't even ask how much I wanted for it and said "I'll give you twelve hundred pounds for it", well I nearly danced on the bonnet, but didn't want to lose any value off the price. With that money I could go to Mexico with my best friends and still have two hundred pounds towards spending money. It was the best start I could have wished for and immediately I felt I was in the hands of fate. So I paid my cash to Barry to secure my place and had a great weekend with my mates before preparing for a long trip to work on Monday.

Monday soon arrived and at 6am I was reluctantly out of the house and embarking on my epic journey for a gruelling day at the office whilst nursing a hangover. I couldn't wait for the return journey, not just to end the working day but to figure out the quickest and exact route, in the rain that is. Although it was now almost August the summer weather was quite depressing, all the more reason to look forward to some holiday sunshine. When I eventually arrived home it was seven thirty pm, I had some student type dinner which usually consisted of something on toast or a microwave meal usually kept for Friday or Saturday, then a quick wash and change ready for the 'Monday Night Club'.

The MNC has been an important part of my life since about

the age of twenty. It was when some of the school gang would meet to do the pub quiz, it was actually an excuse to break up the working week and have a few beers. It helps the weekend drinking blend with the oncoming working week and bridges the gap before Thursday night's football game and a few beers afterwards, which in turn warms up nicely for Friday night and again ready for Saturday's football game and many beers to follow after working up a good sweat. When I say football I do mean British football or soccer as it also known around the globe; however I refuse to call it soccer as the origin of the game came way before American football, the two sports must never be confused and correct names should be applied always, just so you know.

The usual suspects would meet at the local pub just two minutes walk from home. We would meet at about an hour before the quiz at nine thirty and have a couple of beers and discuss the weekend's events before beginning to engage our brains for some serious intellectual stimulus. We always maintained the same team name 'The Bean Flickers' and generally squabbled over the answer to each question before then re-addressing the quiz master to check what order the answers should be in, too busy talking and laughing out loud to take it too seriously.

The prize for winning the quiz was a gallon of ale, so if we ever won it would add another hour onto our evening. If we lost, which was more often than not, we would stay and drink anyway and put the world to rights until we were asked to leave. We always ended up talking about cooking or food which is a bad thing after eight pints of fizzy lager. The quiz night has always been looked down upon with the wives and girlfriends, maybe because it was men only but they wouldn't enjoy it anyway talking pure rubbish, swilling ale amid a fog of cigarette smoke [until the recent ban]. In the early days one or two of the lads would bring their better halves to witness for themselves the glamour of the MNC, needless to say none ever made a return visit.

So this particular MNC was all talk about the holiday and the excitement was building nicely. I must admit I didn't know that much about Mexico at that time. My knowledge extended to Hugo Sanchez and World cup '86, Cactus, Donkeys, cliff divers, Azteca stadium, Tequila, Earthquakes, Sombreros, oh and Herbie goes bananas. I know it sounds ignorant but I'm being truthful that's all. So a holiday there was something really exciting, I don't think any of the others knew a great deal more than me. There just isn't any exposure to Latin America culture in the sleepy town of Preston, Lancashire ["Now a City" as my Dad barks] I am maybe painting a loutish picture of my friends and I but if truth be known we are actually quite a cultured bunch, excluding an extended knowledge of Latin America that is. I'd say we were somewhere between snobbish and regular young gents, certainly not estate boys.

The next few weeks flew by and I had shed some excess weight from all the summer football and a diet of beans on toast not to mention the added exercise I had from running for buses. If it wasn't for a regular Sunday roast with the lads and Wednesday night at mums I wouldn't have all my nutrients for the week. I managed to scrape together a pitiful four hundred pounds for my total spending money which was to last for fourteen nights in the Caribbean. The added bonus was that the hotel would be classed as all inclusive with as much food and booze as you could take in, just a ten hour flight to contend with first.

Chapter 2

Pleased to meet you

The early start didn't bother any of us because it meant we would arrive mid afternoon in Mexico with the six hour difference, so straight on the beer in the sunshine was the plan. We all met outside the pub at six am ready for the mini bus to take us to Manchester airport, this is usually one of the most exciting parts of any trip because everyone is still fresh and not yet feeling the effects from travelling, it also highlighted our childish sides as we joked around and the mass laughter soon started at each others silly jokes.

The biggest laugh didn't take long to arrive when James said during a brief silence "So, where are we off to? "We all fell about pissing our sides. Somebody asked what he had told his family about where he was going for two weeks; his reply was "I'm off on holiday, see you later". The thought of no smoking for ten hours gave us solidarity but not much else; it surely isn't natural to be kept in such a small space in one position for so long? Then again my brother Ian his wife Anne who lived in Australia had made numerous visits to England and that was with three young children, so I had nothing really to moan about travelling with this motley crew did I?

I've never been a great flyer as my lack of wings has always let me down. I don't really mind short flights around Europe; anything under three hours is perfect for me. I actually really like taking off and landing especially if it is during day light so you can watch through the window; my only real fear is that of the dreaded turbulence. As far as I'm concerned turbulence should be banned and I actually suspect it is a ploy by the airlines just to get everyone in their seats so the attendants can get on and do their jobs more easily. I mean it's not much different to being on a bumpy road in a car, well actually you don't drop one hundred feet usually popping to the shop for a small white loaf but the concept of pockets of air change is fairly disturbing to me.

My sister's husband Gaz also shares my beliefs in what we call VTB [visit the bog] it gets under your skin knowing that at any moment the seat belt signs are going to flash and everyone scurries back to their seats, or in our case for a pretend shit! It somehow feels safer in there, as though you are untouchable, that is until the stewardess comes and knocks on the door ordering you back to your seat for the fifth time.

The flight got underway and was actually not to bad at all, I mean after all we had still the excitement of being on holiday, best friends all together, making jokes, passing round newspapers, playing cards, drinking beer etc but then the second hour of the flight became a bit of a drag. Both John and I have always had a strong case of LET [Low Embarrassment Threshold] so if any of the group dropped a swear word or much worse, wind then we would cringe for the surrounding passengers and families on the plane, this combined with being crammed in like cattle with virtually no room to lift your arm to take a drink was getting all a bit too much. Even listening to Paul tell us how he hates onions, even if they are concealed in an elaborate dish was too wearing a bit thin.

He actually has a phobia about onions and wherever he goes for a meal he demands 'no salad' which is often a location of concealed onion, plus salad didn't really appeal to him or people less than thirty years of age for some reason. So after a forty minute period of VTB, two plastic meals and some sentimental garbage movies we eventually were preparing to land, the time had come to have it large!

Five hours later after getting through customs with the correct papers filled out all signed in the right box and one two hour coach trip later we did eventually pull into our budget hotel. If you've never known Cancun imagine a sunset strip of beach front hotels, very much like say Miami but with a Mexican and Latin influence, it was impressive to say the least. All the hotels apart from ours were plush five star abodes likened to ones I've never seen before, it really was an exciting journey through the hotel zone seeing the place we had two weeks to drink dry. We were all obviously single on this particular trip as we had to leave the others behind and boys being boys we were all quite willing to have some female company, as we were all big fans of the opposite sex.

I was actually just glad I made the trip to be honest because four weeks previously I was almost keeping the car and spending my summer holiday punching the clown home alone. I had no real need to complicate my peaceful holiday by chasing women until all hours of the night just to have half a chance of a shag, I was much more relaxed than many of the others as I had broken up recently and in the time before the holiday I had two short term relationships and really needed to clear my head, not to complicate it more. Well not unless it was laid on a plate, so to speak.

We realised the coach trip was taking so long because our hotel was at the very end of the hotel zone, almost in downtown Cancun city. No real problem with that but you could almost see the guys calculating the hotel hopping later in the holiday as they chased women around for some fun and frolics adding to the logistical nightmare that it would impose. We were all sizing out the place, finding our bearings like where is the bar, the best beach, how to catch the bus or taxi to the hot spots and where to change money, all the important things to be taken into account before getting to pissed to realise which way was home.

We had also arranged to meet Jim's brother, Harry and a couple of his mates who were all jetting in from Philadelphia the same day. I have to say Harry's mates were an absolute scream, some of the funniest guys I'd ever met and always willing to party, big time. Jim and Harry had been to the same resort within the last year on a previous trip and the brother's reports would have put the Saxon's to shame.

Jim had already been in Philadelphia with Harry when they took that particular flight and Jim was seated next to a lovely American guy who befriended him as they spent most of the journey discussing each others life stories. Jim happened to mention the game of cricket in conversation and the guy was intrigued to hear more detail of the Gentleman's game. Jim proceeded to tell in full how the game could last up to three days and how two men batted whilst eleven others fielded. The guy was enthralled and had looked astonished when Jim explained how the players broke for lunch and a cup of hot tea. It was only at the end of Jim's twenty minute insight into the game when he knew his new best friend hadn't fully grasped the rules as he enquired "Shit, they do all that on horse back"?

Both Jim and Harry are or were masters of pulling women, when all the rest of us stand there in a club looking like we'd just learned how to join sentences, Jim and Harry could easily just hold a profiled look at the opposite sex and they'd be starting the taxi outside. Anyway we had drawn straws for room sharing and I had been drawn with Jim and we had been assigned the smallest room.

Through his excitement Harry had found himself not booked into the hotel with his American friends and had also bypassed the arranging of booking into our hotel, so he ending up sharing with Jim and me on a mattress on the floor. This was fine by me but to have the pressure of the Brothers renowned ability to drink until the sun comes up added to the flocks of women that would be tailing behind would be a test of endurance to say the least. I had the choice either to bite the bullet and try and keep up with them or curl up in a ball and suck my thumb. I believe things happen for a reason and I've always believed in fate, so no need to be WLF [worried like fuck} after all sharing with Jim alone has always been an absolute blast, we are best buddies any way along with Nick and Baz, or the Fab four as we have been known to call ourselves. All of the group are best buddies but the four of us have always been as close as brothers and all four being on the trip was enough for me, never mind trying to keep up with the rest of them I would be happy to coast along and see what happens.

It's funny because the older you get the less resistance or actual desire to be out clubbing all night diminishes with every year, many of our group on the trip were beginning to go through the change. I know for a fact Barry and in particular Nick would like nothing better to have a slap up evening meal after a day of sunshine, beach football, fishing, beer and watching near naked women all day long then head into town for a couple of hours and if a women hadn't approached and said take me home and ravish me, then they would be on the next bus back to the hotel for a night cap and bed. I would therefore fall into a category somewhere in between owing to my designated 'roomies' track records and my anticipated relaxation programme.

Due to delays in the airport and with the coach ride the day's sunshine had diminished and early evening had suddenly begun. Once in the hotel the plan was to grab a quick shower and meet downstairs at the restaurant for a safety feed before attempting to drink as much free all inclusive alcohol as possible before a quick bus trip into the centre of the hotel zone. As we all ascended into the restaurant looking like Brits abroad, pale as pale can be and easily identified as we were all dressed in a similar way, jeans and short sleeved shirts and all completely wet through with sweat from the shear humidity. What we hadn't banked on was the time of our arrival which was mid August, the most ridiculously hot period in the Caribbean but it was too late now to complain, our only blessing was that at least it wasn't yet hurricane season.

We walked up and down the hotel's evening buffet selection and drooled over what was delicious steak, fish and chicken of every description and all sorts of exotic Mexican dishes full of colour and spices too. We were in heaven but poor Paul was a little upset because almost every thing on the menu was adorned with onions. We all sat down with every type of dish we could get on one plate accompanied with bread rolls of every description and gallons of beer to swill it all down. Going around the table, there was Nick, Nigel, John, Barry, James, Harry, Jim and me, but where had Paul gone? Surely he hadn't gone back to his room without a safety feed; maybe he'd got a taxi and gone to McDonald's? We tried not to laugh but thinking of Paul's two week turmoil made us all the more eager to take the piss. All of a sudden I saw Paul out of the corner of my eye, he was in reception with someone who resembled a hotel manager and Paul was doing his famous 'no salad' gesture which entailed crossing one's a lofted palms twice in the direction of the intended. I was nearly on the floor laughing; the poor guy was 'Hank Marvin' and head to toe in sweat. Before you could say Tequila Paul was sat with us tucking into a plate of plain steak and chips with no salad, no salsa, no trimmings of any kind, normally Paul would see the funny side of events like this but I think the journey, the heat and then the onions was all too much for him, poor guy.

As we soon found out Mexico and I'm sure in the US and many other North and South American countries, tips are not included so it was necessary to carry a small collection of change around everywhere you go and I mean everywhere and tip say ten to fifteen percent which is fair but just a pain in the arse when on holiday and not wanting to be hassled. It is one of the cultural differences between England and the rest of the world, we just include tips in all prices and never even think about it, but when you analyze the reason why it's because much of these countries are suffering from poverty and in Mexico's case up to seventy percent of the population suffers from being in the third world and these people have nothing more than a few dollars in their pockets.

Tips therefore are a lifeline to many of the people you meet. The remainder of the Mexican population is made up of descendants of the Spanish who invaded Mexican shores hundreds of years ago and to this day the divide is still easily recognisable. The people with education, money and materialistic belongings are the ones who you would say look Latin and the poorer people who barely have anything to speak of are more the descendants of the Indian Mexicans who have a very distinctive look. All this cultural history and knowledge was being downloaded rapidly by us all mostly from reading material in the bathroom and we were quickly adapting to this wonderful exotic country and its varied and different way of life. We all thought it was a great idea to come to Mexico but none of us really knew how much we would like it so much and we were amazed at the fabulous warmth of the people, it really was an eye opener at the way they knew how to live to fullest not only that but we were in the Caribbean where Fiesta is not just a Magazine but an every day occurrence.

Nigel had already been studying Spanish on the flight with his little phrase book, straight away he spouted out a few words to a waiter or a local and in his posh accent it would be another reason to be in stitches with laughter. So equipped with approximately a dozen Spanish words and no real idea where we were heading, we retired to the front bar for some free ale. We regretted the fact that we were trying to abuse the system because the front bar was not air conditioned and the temperature was in the thirties, bearing in mind it was now around ten pm. We managed a further two hours drinking when it dawned on us that we were sweating quicker than we could drink and apart from some resident British girls in the restaurant we felt the need to change the scenery and get amongst it, it being people of the skirted variety. We tipped handsomely and crossed the death defying dual carriageway to the nearby bus stop.

The bus was cheap enough, equivalent to two and a half pence each to take us into the main zone about ten minutes away. Whilst on the bus many other people boarded from all over the world, some families, some groups of youths like us and some locals all mixed in. It was brilliant, the way every one fitted together in one happy go lucky kind of way, even the Mariachi with full velvet suit and guitar who boarded didn't seem to mind the sweltering heat. If you've ever heard the Mariachis play it just takes your mind away with the music, I absolutely loved it. It is the kind of music that really makes you feel like you are somewhere exotic and we all got into the swing of the Mexican nightlife, especially as we all had a belly full of ale. So whilst in the town we did the usual bar crawl and sampled a few shots along the way, tequila, um and Bacardi, not really to my taste but stronger than the pissy hotel lager.

The town was absolutely packed to the rafters, we had arrived in peek season and mostly Americans having a blast going wild and as Harry's mates told us this was the main destination during spring and summer breaks for many Americans. The shear volume of classy hotels, bars, shops, malls, restaurants and people of course was outstanding; I've never seen anything quite like it. Some of the nightclubs themselves were as big as Preston where we came from. What seemed like a thousand of people crammed in, dancing from the balconies semi-clad and everyone having a wild time, this was to be some holiday that was for sure.

We ended up in one particular club that took our fancy which had dance podiums all over, two separate floors, numerous bars and more women than you could shake you tail at. The Brothers assumed their position at the balcony and waited like a twin fly catcher plant, the rest of us wandered around drink in hand, which was rapidly becoming spirits and no longer beer as it was not getting us anywhere near drunk due to the heat or so we thought. I decided enough was enough and succumbed to Montezuma's revenge and followed Nigel to the gents, he enabled us to be whisked to the front of the queue by using his pigeon Spanish of "Coming through, my mate's touching cloth" and before I knew it I was in a cubicle consisting of papier-mâché constructed walls and a three foot high door. When I sat down I could see the whole room and more to the point they could see me, a fourteen stone pale faced Englishman in distress. I had had quite enough for one day, it was time to retire and see who else was itching to return, I paid the toilet attendant who assisted me with producing a paper towel from the dispenser [I'll never know how I managed without him] and left to find the gang. Luckily everyone was ready for heading back, apart from my roomies of course so we decided to jump in a taxi to get us back sooner. It was great to return to your own bed on that first night, without being run over on the crazy roads, without having your stomach pumped and without having paid hotel security a hundred dollars to allow you to have access to the beach for a sexual encounter. Some of the guys hung around the hotel bar for some time more because there were the four British girls still sweating their rocks off in reception, for me it was off to bed to reflect on having developed what felt like two leaky arseholes.

The next morning was greeted by a stifled stench of spicy food farts mixed with alcohol, Jim and Harry had made it back safely but only with more tales of heavy drinking, and run ins with hotel security to tell. I was sharing a room with two of the best looking guys around but little did the outside world know was that Jim was the North West champion farter and Harry had been Lancashire's nose picking gold medallist seven years running, it would have been eight but his face had caved in.

We quickly replaced Harry's mattress to Jim's bed so the

maid didn't clock onto that three people were actually staying in the room and bounded down for breakfast which was again greeted by a mound of bread rolls followed by the biggest array of food stuff since I'm not sure what. You name it, you could have it, even beef casserole, and I went for a Mexican breakfast which was spicy scrambled eggs and all the trimmings including onions. Paul had toast and jam, sorry marmalade, he doesn't like jam because of the seeds, but then again he's not so keen of the shred in marmalade but with some nifty knife work that can be easily treated.

Following another fantastic feed it was time to go and play footy on the beach and ogle some women, well we were all single guys for Pete's sake, who is Pete by the way? It couldn't be my brother Pete all the time dispelling my theory of this elusive character. Anyway we all settled in well to the beach footy after all it wasn't the first time we had been away together and we held a captive audience while managing to maintain an almost orderly circle whilst keeping the ball in the air. Following an enlarged toe nail meeting knee accident Nigel retired to apply his eight layers of factor fifty sun lotion [he's not called Milk Bottle Nigel for nothing you know]

Nigel's knee was a real mess with blood pouring from it, it had reached the bone and none of us could bear to look at it. Paul would be having a snooze all oiled up, but shaded, John and me kept playing 'keepy upy' around the pool, Nick would be surveying the fairer sex whilst smoking heavily and breathing heavily come to mention it, Jim, James and Harry would be found checking out the beach bar and the amenities whilst Barry was abstaining from the application of barrier cream, what a bunch we must have looked.

We'd been away in Europe many times where the sun is less strong and although I could see sense in his theory of no cream first day to get bedded in, I just couldn't understand the six hours on a sun bed right through the middle of the day in the middle of August in Mexico, with no protection. The next morning was greeted by "Don't fucking touch me" as his shoulder blisters glistened in the morning light like huge barnacles.

After a superb day of fun and games round the pool, with another impressive game of 'keepy upy', watching semi naked girls play volleyball, drinking free beer, having delicious Mexican food buffet style all day and soaking up the sun we could have easily been in heaven. If nothing changed for the whole two weeks we would have been happy enough with what we had.

The hotel activity staff were excellent and they endured a lot of flack from us especially when we were all lined up in beach beds along the volleyball court goggle eyed at the promotional girls in skimpy thongs bearing flesh, whilst jigging up and down I may add. The next few days passed much the same and we inevitably became immune to the sight of a near naked women, I think it's one of those natural developments that once it becomes a formality it then becomes a lot less interesting but later in the evening when you spot a girl with a skimpy blouse bearing a glimpse of bra strap then it suddenly awakens the demon inside.

Most of the next few nights were spent at the same bars and clubs and things had started to become a little bit much of the same so other than eat at the buffet we pushed the boat out and ate at the adjacent al la carte restaurant. We paid a supplement but it was more than worth it, they had beach barbeques with the freshest, nicest fish you've ever tasted. Nick asked the Mexican waiter serving from the beach barbeque grill what type of fish it was as he handed over his plate. The waiter's response brought the house down, Fish or Feeesh but pronounced with a heavy bandit twang.

It was at this point that Nick decided to play the 'Arsehole' joke on our poor table waiter. "Ah sole, my favourite", scoring one. "Are soles in season"? he asked, by now all the little boys were in fits. "These are arseholes aren't they"? Scoring three, we couldn't take it any more and requested Nick to leave it there.

We also enjoyed playing our own version of Celebrity Squares whilst eating our meal, we were pool side and facing the hotel rooms and balconies, many a night we saw Barbara Windsor mid towel dry. We had all suffered somehow from unwelcome bowel activity however, during one game of Celebrity Squares James casually rose to his feet and announced he was to depart to his room for a dump, he calmly navigated the pool edge and rounded his way towards the lift area where he suddenly turned into Carl Lewis, bounded through the hedgerow and disappeared to rapturous applause. On returning he announced embarrassedly "It was like shit through a goose".

The idea of another night drinking weak piss like beer or even spirits whilst sweating through the humidity was beginning to become a drag, we needed another direction or even just to slacken the pace a little. Maybe we should have a night in like the boring old farts we really are. Well maybe one more night then, let's see who had played their trump cards and who would get lucky with the ladies.

Nigel was leading the proceedings with the book of sin, he had every ones daily report on how many women they'd enjoyed the company of, how many had visited second and third base and how many times one had enjoyed the company of Pamela and her five sisters. Nick had shot straight to the top of the chart on one column as he'd hardly been out of his room, I think someone had told him that his life depended on it and he was more than happy to lend a hand.

The book that Nigel was keeping also recorded the jokers being played; everyone had one joker and played it on an evening when they saw fit. It basically entailed a small piece of card depicting a fake joker and its function was to spur on the owner to make contact with a woman and increase the chances of success with chat up lines and to do things you wouldn't normally have the courage to do. Although the book was revealing a few guys had GFE [Gone Fat Early] to boost their score, one of them said that the girl in question had lovely skin; the problem was she had lots of it! A few had also squandered their jokers, I was quite happy to keep mine for a later date and tag along in awe of the organised womanising that was unfolding before my eyes.

I have never been gifted at delivering chat up lines, I guess you need that extra bit of confidence to go out there and flaunt yourself, the exact reason why Nigel produced the record book and joker system, otherwise we would all be sat around looking at each other for two weeks with nothing more than a sun tan to show for it. I did make a feeble attempt at delivering a line at the pool one day, Paul and I were soaking up the intense rays as two girls walked slowly past, it was time to unleash the love god in me and I said "Is it warm enough for you"? The girls carried on walking without saying a word as Paul rolled around his sun bed holding his beak.

The holiday was going great but the strain was beginning to tell on a few of the lads, I know Baz and Nick were finding it difficult to sustain the clubbing until early morning especially after a gruelling day playing beach football in the hundred degrees heat. So for a change a night around the pool bar was lined up whilst John, Paul, Nigel and James pursued with keeping up with the main protagonists in the centre of town. After another great meal and some fine hotel entertainment Baz, Nick and I chilled around the pool bar where there was a breeze to ease the sweltering heat, we chatted about life in general and drank and smoked a decent amount whilst doing it.

We spotted the four English girls who had returned from a day trip somewhere and began chatting, Nick was ruing having not played his joker but Nigel was in town with his little book of tricks, maybe he wouldn't need it as he seemed to be doing alright without it.

Myself and Baz sat back and watched as Nick worked his magic on the girls, to be honest we just couldn't summons enough enthusiasm to lend a hand, it was almost as if we had run out of get up and go, we were both fairly recently out of long term relationships and like I said unless some girl sat on our knee and tampered with our zip we were happy to just press on with enjoying the freedom we had whilst savouring a fine glass of red wine for a nice change. If truth be known I'd opt for a glass of red any day before a beer but I think that just comes with age I suppose.

The English girls were all very pretty but nothing that spurred me on to try anything, just to have a laugh with and be thoroughly decent along the way. We as a whole group though, which includes all the many guys who didn't come on the trip due to having wives or girlfriends, can be very mean when it comes to conjuring up names or character references for girls we meet. It is very childish I know but extremely good fun all the same.

The four English girls were no exception and were given character names the following morning around breakfast with the group. If you've ever heard holiday laughter it always sounds more energetic as though the laugh has been brought from your boots, what I mean is especially when you've had a lot to drink the night before and have a hangover or after a full day at the beach and early evening before a shower you are always more susceptible to a proper belly laugh. Well the naming of the girls was another example of proper belly laughing from nine men spitting spicy breakfast accidentally across the table, apart from one who had toast and marmalade. The girls secretly adopted names were; Margot [from the good life], Aunt Sally [from Worzel Gummidge], Oscar the grouch [from Sesame Street] and last but not least Jar Jar Binks [from Star Wars] Poor girls, they were pretty but didn't escape our childish ritual.

Nick and Margot hit it off right from the start and began a daily routine of bashing uglies. It looked like Nick had the title licked already with only a week gone, the tension at the top of the league was nail biting. We all sat around the pool one afternoon wondering what was actually going on in Nick's room as they had again been at it all day, Jim shouted up towards the direction of the room "If they're not careful they're going to break that coffee table". Meanwhile I was propping up the rear of the league, but I didn't mind at all, I was having a splendid time with a lot of splendid chaps and I strangely knew somehow I was on some kind of journey.

I mean it was fate that I had sold my car and fate would deal me a good hand when the time was right. The fact that on returning to England the weather would be worsening for my epic commuting to work didn't deter me or the fact that my cash was rapidly running out. Maybe I could borrow a few hundred pounds from one of the lads and pay them back next time I got paid, anyone who has an all inclusive deal at a hotel and thinks they won't need much spending money is fooling themselves. Somehow you can always manage to haemorrhage money whilst enjoying yourself.

Due to a momentary cash flow crisis and the knowledge that heavy seas will cause violent sickness I declined the fishing trip that had been arrange for the whole day, instead I decided to stay by the pool, read a book, have a few beers and hang out with our new female companions. The rest of the group shelled out eighty dollars each to head miles out into the Caribbean ocean for some deep sea fishing. It would entail approximately eight hours of concentrating on the horizon whilst attempting not to be sick through your nose; I was quite happy with my deal and headed to the buffet for the second time in short succession.

The day past at a nice slow pace but eventually I watched as the hire boat worked it's way back to shore, the first thing I noticed when the lads trundled down the jetty was that most of them looked as if they had been to a place that only they knew what horrific events had occurred. It was only until I chatted with Jim who seemed the liveliest of all I got the whole story of what had actually happened. After only one hour at sea five of the group were nestled inside the boat for the remaining seven hours huddled together in their fight against seasickness, making regular breaks to the edge were spicy Mexican breakfast was regurgitated via nasal alleyways.

Jim, Harry and Paul on the other hand had managed to keep their insides to themselves and enjoyed a spot of fishing with the two guides. The ability to remain calm was mostly due to the fact Jim had hooked what they thought was huge Marlin, so the next few hours were spent hauling it in and capturing the final process on video. When the huge fish was onboard Jim nonchalantly turned to the camera and added "I used to fish for Lancashire you know".

After a night of recovering in their rooms the gang re-convened at breakfast, the date now being 18/08/2000, I am slightly superstitious and my lucky number has always been eighteen or anything with the number eight in general. It follows me every where I go and still amazes me to this day how I can be somewhere and these numbers keep popping up from nowhere. When I turned eighteen the actual date was 18/12/88 and I always remember my brother Pete giving me a gold chain from Saudi Arabia where he had been working and of course it was eighteen carats on my eighteenth birthday on 18/12/88, [ignore the 12, I did] I always held the chain as a good luck charm from this point on in.

It's all a bit silly I know but these superstitions sometimes can't be helped and always happen on their own accord from somewhere beyond our control. When I bought my first house, you guessed it, it was number eighteen again by pure chance and there were many more similar occasions where again the numbers appear.

With the days date firmly fixed in my mind I wondered maybe if God does really answer your prayers. I am a Catholic and I had the usual upbringing of being an altar boy for ten years and then ditching going to Church at the age of sixteen because it was what young men did. But I have always since spoken to God and asked occasional favours which sometimes worked out for me, I had already been gifted with a great life to date so I had no reason to doubt my faith even if it was only the odd prayer. So armed with my lucky eighteen and my faith I decided to play my joker at long last, with four nights remaining of the holiday and Friday night beckoning it was a decision I will never forget.

We followed our usual routine after showering, having dinner and playing celebrity squares then retired to the sauna like front bar and raced against sweat and alcohol consumption. Ten days into the holiday and Nigel's Spanish vocabulary had increased ten fold and he had prepared a hat full of phrases for us all to pick from and utilise as a fun introduction. John and Baz had also played their awaited jokers and picked from the hat some local ditty that would stand them in good stead later in the evening.

It was my turn to pick from the hat and I opened the scrap piece of paper to reveal my Spanish phrase 'Mucho Gusto' which translates as 'Pleased to meet you'. I was all set for a great night, I felt very reassured that evening and had a feeling in the back of my mind that I was being guided a certain way and as the evening progressed all I had to do was follow the signs. It sounds a bit strange and possibly corny but what can I say, that's exactly how it felt to me.

We took a group vote not to jump on a bus into town this particular evening but to visit the huge nightclub right across the road or the race track road as we had christened it. The club was called 'La Boom' and although we kind of knew it was always there, we never gave it a thought because we had been so used to the multiple bars and clubs in the centre and didn't think one place for the whole evening would be enough for our needs.

As the holiday was two thirds in and many of the group were showing their age or non desire to party until you couldn't wait to be tucked up in bed, this evening's plan was greeted with a unanimous thumbs up. After all if it didn't work out as planned then the bus was right outside for town and for anyone wanting to retire to bed or to bribe security to allow a girl to share your retirement, it was a quick sprint back across the race track.

As we entered La Boom we all looked at each other in disbelief, the place was inundated with beautiful Latina girls all stunning looking with their silky black hair and healthy mocha glow, a very welcome change from the mixed bunch in town we all thought. We were out numbered by women by three to one; you would have to work very hard indeed not to have any degree of success in this particular club, in fact even Quasimodo could have scored.

The club was enormous, much bigger than it looked from the outside and it was split into two sections, one was playing excellent dance music and the other smaller section had a bar that people, mostly girls, were dancing on and playing rap music. Both were fantastic and you felt as if you had a change of scenery every half hour or so. We all agreed that this place was rocking, it was after all just what the doctor ordered and proceeded to top up our drinks and began having the best night so far all together as one group. As time pushed on and the drinks flowed we switched bars and gradually got split into smaller formations and simply followed the music, the crowds of people and the gorgeous girls.

The night wore on and we eventually all grouped back together in the larger section which was now reaching boiling point and pumping out really good music. None of us were dance music clubbers but we all knew good tunes when we heard them and just couldn't resist the brilliant sound magnifying itself around the room. We had been treated to good music all week and as all good summers and holidays go there were always holiday favourites like Spiller Grove-Jet 'why does it feel so good' and Modjo 'Lady' which were playing everywhere you turned. At this point the DJ played another summer favourite Darude 'Sandstorm' and we danced like crazy to it, when I looked around everyone of us was going mental even those who don't usually dance and those who can't, including me was having a proper boogie.

There is a point during the track were the music goes soft and then builds to an enormous crescendo of techno sounds and the sound system was not only the best I'd ever heard but also the loudest, we all stood on our perched balcony and soaked up the moment. For me it was almost spiritual, I can't quite describe it but it was almost like being purged, I felt on top of the world and again I thought maybe I was guided to this high for I certainly wasn't completely drunk and who needs drugs when you can reach a high like we all had.

It was so difficult to become drunk or on your way to being drunk like in England after say five pints of beer you feel that tingle feeling, in Mexico with the heat and the excessive sweating I think you had to drink spirits to maintain any kind of tingle. My point I'm trying to make is that at all times you always were in control and never falling down drunk as with so many degenerates you see all around, we all kept a certain amount of dignity, well that was until I saw Nigel in one of the podium boxes with a beautiful girl doing the 'hands crossing knees' dance, it was his speciality.

You could tell by everyone's faces that they were enjoying the night so much that no one was going to town or back to the hotel until we were thrown out right at closing time. There was still about three hours left and three jokers had being played, we weren't going anywhere just yet. As I gazed across the slightly lower level I spotted a group of what looked like well to do locals on a night out, there were four girls and two guys all dancing and having fun. One of the girls caught my eye immediately, I looked hard at her face as she chatted away oblivious at this stage to my interest.

Her face looked familiar, or did it? I was unsure; one thing I knew was that she had the most beautiful face I'd ever seen. I looked on some more whilst in my private bubble, this girl had me in a trance, I was hoping that by chance she would turn and look at me so maybe I should get closer but my feet wouldn't move, I was scared stiff. Like I'd said I've never been the worlds best at chatting up girls but I wasn't prepared to let this girl leave tonight without me at least making contact somehow, maybe I should throw some ice over her way and just make it glance her ear? I really didn't know what to do and decided to bide my time and keep my eyes pinned on her and her only. I'm sorry but even if I needed a piss, I was prepared to pipe it into the pocket of whoever was standing next to me; I was like a crouching tiger waiting to pounce.

It was almost as if it was a vision that I was following yet still I was trying to make direct eye contact with her, then eventually it happened. I didn't want to look creepy but again didn't want to loose this angelic girl forever, I had to think fast and devise a plan. I stepped out of my bubble briefly and told some of the guys around about my quest, the general consensus was go for it or forever regret it, Nick said "Oh my god, you must go and talk to her, just go, I'll hold your drink and fags". But still my legs wouldn't budge, she was in deep conversation with her friends and I was beginning to feel that all my staring was maybe freaking her out, until her friends also turned around and were staring back, as were my friends in turn to them.

This was getting silly, the entire eye to eye contact stage had taken more than two hours now can you believe, but still I was in control, or someone else above was more like. It was no good I had to make my move; I charged forward ten steps and began my decent with numerous back slapping encouragement from the others. It was all in vein, as I approached a middle aged guy with a naff Hawaiian shirt on whisked her away to the dance floor, as she was spun around our eyes met again, she looked as though she really didn't want to dance with him and it gave us chance to exchange a brief smile.

I dashed back to my position and desperately tried to locate the wanker that was edging closer to his last breath but couldn't see anything amongst the mass of people, I could however see her friends and knew she would be returning to them and settled knowing the song would finish soon. The club was also soon to finish
, I had to think fast, it suddenly dawned on me I had my ticket from Nigel; I could use it as my first line as she returned from the dance floor. Perfect, but where was it I thought as I fumbled around in my pockets and what did it say again?

Eventually from the crowd of clubbers her face appeared once more and more perfect it became the more I gazed on, she walked towards her friends and gestured that she was going to powder her nose, this meant I just needed to be in her way as she walked passed, my one and only chance had arrived. She got closer and closer and eventually close enough for me to gently grasp her arm, enough for her to turn right round so we were face to face, then I remembered my line or at least I thought I did. "Mucho Gambo" is said, she replied with "what"? The music was very loud, I thought maybe I didn't say it loud enough "Mucho Gambo" I bellowed in her ear. [It was later I found out that I had made a bizarre reference to much casserole from Brazil]

She brushed my mistake aside and we exchanged pleasantries in English of course, we immediately felt at ease chatting away, well we did already have two and a half hours head start. We swiftly addressed the usual subjects such as family, work and hobbies and found we had a lot in common apart from she had never been a pipe fitter welder, not to date any way. I was offered a glass of champagne from Sairel whose birthday it was and as I raised the glass to my lips, I turned to face the balcony behind me revealing eight thumbs up as my friends looked on in amazement.

We were both Catholic, both had three middle names, both the youngest of a large family and both loved football, which lead me to a little white lie, well I was playing my joker so over egging the truth couldn't be avoided. I said I was a semi-professional footballer back in England, in fact I said we all were but truthfully we all played for a very un-professional amateur team except for John who was actually semi pro with FA cup experience under his belt.

I didn't feel too bad about my manipulation of the truth because I had played a couple of pre-season friendly games for John's team along with Jim, because they were short of course, so it wasn't entirely untrue due to a minor technicality. Nonetheless I got away with it and as time was pressing on we realised that people were beginning to be ushered out of the club so we slowly edged our way out also, maybe her visit to the ladies was also a neatly conjured ploy.

I had finally met someone out of the blue who took my breath away and I knew we would meet again to continue what had seemed like a meeting arranged by fate; I couldn't for the life of me though catch her name. As she pronounced her name for the fifth time we gave up, it sounded Mayan or at least a name I just couldn't register so instead she told me her second name Viviana. She also told me by coincidence that one of her best friends from school now lived in London and she was going to visit her in October, only ten weeks away, we agreed we should definitely keep in touch so as to make contact in England, this again sounded to me like we had already started something, I mean I was blown away right from the beginning.

She hastily wrote her first name Yecora followed by her work telephone number, home and mobile numbers on a serviette, in eyeliner. That was it, I had all I needed, I just knew I was guided to this point and all I had to do was follow the illuminated signs. There was never any question that the evening would continue elsewhere with any slap and tickle involved, it just wasn't like that, we knew and understood each other right away and I knew this was to be no quick lustful holiday relationship, maybe the nuns habit gave it away!

In England it would be polite to plant a small peck on the lips to a girl you had just met when saying good night, equal to say base -2, base -1 being to only look at the bra strap! In Mexico a small peck on the lips is construed as fourth base and not to be attempted until at least you had a couple of year's marriage under your belt. It's funny because as with every country there are girls who are more inclined to take there time and those who are just more inclined, I had found what I thought was a match made in heaven. Although I didn't realise it at the time but the kiss had been bordering on assault as I had seen Yecora and her friends giggling wildly as they walked to their car.

On the other side of the coin, Baz and John were escorting two young ladies from the club that they had selected to initiate whatever they could during their joker playing time. They had earlier indicated their distain at the breath owned by the two girls and likened it with a steaming horse stable, this was purely an obstacle that could be dealt with by adopting swift rules before any clothes were to be removed, the only problem was that these girls were more Mayan Indians than Mexican and they had little or no English to their name.

The guys were not to be beaten by small insignificant things like this and instead of inviting the girls to the hotel beach to carry on the party, they decided to club together and splash out on a swanky penthouse suite in a nearby five star hotel, this after all would cement the deal surely and they would be knee deep in nakedness within the hour, or at least that was the bargain they had thought they had made clear in broken Spanish. John, being the least drunk and the more sensible, stashed both their wallets under the fridge, he must have read some book sometime where two English guys were mugged, stripped and slashed from ear to ear in a bungled holiday spunkathon. Careful John, we called him.

Following a long and meaningless group conversation it became apparent to John and now Barry also that their efforts were in vein and not the blue one! The girls were oblivious to the reason for the over spending of these two British guys before them, they were be all means having a great time but like many of the local girls they were in no way ready to bed with these two strange men. This came as a crushing blow to the guys and between them they slowly, calmly but quite audibly reiterated "This" [pointing at the splendour of the room] "This, has cost us" [us, now pointing at each other] "A lot of money". The girls smiled politely and crossed their legs as the guys plotted a way to achieve some satisfaction to match their expenditure, Baz somehow managed the worlds first forcible pant wank whilst John gave up defeated and casually scooped up the hidden wallets. The girls soon left quite bemused by the whole affair and the guys thought about staying the whole night in their newly acquired room but both agreed to retreat to their other rooms through fear of being mistaken for a rich gay couple at breakfast time.

After boring Jim and Harry to sleep with tales of my evening with this girl called Yecora we eventually woke and I couldn't wait to call her, just to see if she also had the spiritual connection that I felt, I was to play it cool though and see if the next meeting would flow as the first.

It was Saturday morning and at ten am sharp and I rang the home number written on the serviette, after three rings a ladies voice answered and I asked for Yecora although pronounced a little better than my previous attempts "Who is calling"? the lady asked, "My name is David" I replied, "Ah, I hear of you" she said, I had worked out that this was Yecora's mother I was speaking to and I also worked out that in the very short time between our meeting and this conversation, Yecora had told her mother about me, this was a positive start. Yecora came to the phone and we hit it off again straight away as if we had met before, what I mean is, as if we weren't just strangers. We arranged for a lunch time meeting in a nearby downtown shopping mall which went by the name of Liverpool, of all the names, I actually support them, the football team that is, not the retail chain.

I had time to make the obligatory call home like you do and let my parents know I was still alive and kicking, they sounded pleased to hear from me and that I was having a good time, I didn't mention Yecora at the time as it was only a brief call and anyway my dad did most of the talking. Apparently my company back home had been in the news and they announced that were making nine hundred people redundant nationwide. I was obviously concerned about my position but fate would deal me what ever it felt was right so although our office may be disappearing something optimistically would always come up, why worry? After the call I returned to the hotel, relaxed by the pool and contemplated my future then got ready and told the guys about my date, they all seemed really pleased and wished me luck, maybe I would make an entry in Nigel's book after all, if he had a category for hand holding that was!

The taxi dropped me outside the mall at three pm as arranged, the heat was absolutely incredible especially after a late and boozy night before and I was beginning to feel a bit under the weather, so to speak. Twenty minutes passed but I knew I hadn't been stood up, just some kind of delay, or maybe she was just one of those girls that were always late. Any way, as I turned I saw her approach and I immediately fell under her spell again, I just couldn't believe I had only just met her, she looked so familiar or just somehow right, I wasn't sure, I just knew I was already totally amazed by this beautiful angel before me.

Yecora lead me inside the mall entrance which was the coolest, air conditioned entrance I have ever had the pleasure of and she enquired why I hadn't waited inside, we laughed as I was unable to come up with a reasonable answer and I caught sight of the loveliest smile I have ever seen, it was the most powerful smile that you could imagine, enough to make me stare in complete amazement.

This particular kind of human interaction is so rare and unique, so it is without effort that you both communicate and find out more about one another with fascination. It was so easy to get along when all the forces are pulling together like that, we both had a pretty good idea that something special had just begun, even though she was twenty minutes late!.

Natalia a friend of Yecora's walked by and introduced herself; she was the manager of a cool bar and suggested we meet there later that night. We both knew I had only three nights remaining and so we did arrange to go clubbing that night with some more of her friends along with mine. Our first date was now completed with ease and we made secure plans to meet at ten pm at the bar half way in to the town centre.

The guys agreed to spend the last Saturday night in town and visit this new bar that I was to meet Yecora at, all the plans seemed to be falling into place quite splendidly. We spent our usual preparation time in the hotel and made for the bus journey at nine thirty prompt. We were all seated on the bus when It made a routine stop and about ten American girls boarded, one short one, one tall one, one ginger, one with bog eyes, there was one of every type you could imagine.

Nobody made a sound, we all just watched quietly as they made their way passed and to their seats, there was an audible silence throughout that lasted for an age, all it wanted was someone to make a comment, it's not often these moments come about and John wasn't going to miss it for the world. "It's Paul's past" he shouted, even the bus driver howled even though he wasn't sure what he was laughing about. We arrived at the bar which was great, another place we wished we'd found earlier in the holiday but by eleven fifteen when all the lads were ribbing me that Yecora had stood me up, Natalia tapped me on the shoulder and assured me Yecora was on her way, I knew it all along, Yecora was a 'latey'. When she did arrive and gave all the guys a mandatory peck on the cheek, they soon shut up, they were also taken back by her wonderful charm not to mention her captivating smile.

We moved onto the club were I met more of Yecora's friends and we again all had a brilliant night. Maybe things were going too well, I was thinking about the short time we had and still being oblivious to the kissing code I launched into a passionate kiss which I have to say was special and memorable to this day. Each small step we made was unbelievably spellbinding which to us both was making us more aware that this wasn't just any old courtship but a moment in our lives that we would never forget. It never even entered my head that we were going to jump into bed together at any point soon, we had this connection but it wasn't a fling, so we had all the time in the world for things of that nature.

Next day being Sunday we arranged a four pm meeting for

just the two of us at an open air mall next to the lagoon, we walked and talked for hours and settled on a bench overlooking the lagoon and watched the sun set. A nearby bar played Duran Duran 'Save a prayer' quietly in the background as we gazed across the open water. Our conversations again flowed with ease and the subject of conversation leaned into talk about us and what we had begun. By this time there was no doubt that we felt a special bond and had to continue this even after I returned to England.

I could almost hear myself whisper "This might be the girl I've always dreamed off" and to be honest I've never been a soppy kind who goes on about love, marriage and life in that way, but I suppose these things happen when you least expect it. In times gone by there used to be another code, the "Will you be my girlfriend" code, but I know in England it rarely gets said anymore, well at least not outside school age anyway, so it never dawned on me to say anything, I just let the moment develop on its own accord.

We had a brilliant time that Sunday together and discussed meeting up In England in a couple of month's time; it really was an exciting and precious moment. We still had a few hours to spare and then something happened that had been a million miles away from anything I had ever contemplated, we went to the cinema! The cinemas in England are dirty horrible places and at most you would go once a year, however in this part of the world the cinemas are plush, well staffed and even have VIP leather reclining seats, a totally different standard all together and they are all air conditioned.

The majority of the population went to the cinema at least twice a month and it was big business. Anyway as I was totally un-used to this type of entertainment just like the rest of the group so I would expect some ribbing from the lads at breakfast, I could almost hear them saying "So, did you remove her bra"? "No we went to the cinema instead" etc etc. I enjoyed the date so much I now had the cinema bug unlike my dad who's last film at the cinema was Pretty Women and when asked if he enjoyed the parts he hadn't slept through he said "No, it was bloody rubbish". On our way to my hotel we planned our last evening together in Mexico, well at least for the time being.

We were to go for a meal together at a posh Mexican restaurant in town, Yecora was to pick me up at nine pm, God willing and we would take it from there. Our flight was the following morning and already the guys were setting about for their last night's activities. We had a great day on the beach topping up our tans and had to laugh when we witnessed James and Nick judging a children's sand castle competition, they had been roped into it by the staff because they were lounging directly in the way of the event and the staff decided to involve them instead of ejecting them. When we asked who had won between some local kids and the foreigners James replied dead pan faced in front of everyone "The Mexicans, they had a fucking moat"

We trudged off the beach and towards our rooms to get showered and changed, I was obviously excited as this was to be the biggest night of my life, it's not every day you think you've met the women of your dreams and then you fly four and a half thousand miles in the opposite direction. We approached reception to the lifts and were met by an arrangement of temporary English and Spanish signs, Baz yelled from in front to us all tailing behind "The water's off until midnight for repairs", it was then that eight of my friends became hysterical with laughter, they all knew it was a big night for me and they could see my eyes glaze over as I absorbed the news and became WLF once again.

Jim was especially un-supportive and had to hold his nose for laughing as he rolled on his bed at the sight of me frantically washing my sandy arse in the sink with what drops of water there were left. I think it was the initial sight of my dangling feet from his vantage point that set him off, but it wasn't helping. It was too late to go and dive in the pool, which would only anger the smell of chlorine anyway, it was nearing nine o'clock and I had to get downstairs quickly, being British it was the only way to be, on time.

With a pocket full of borrowed money and half a bottle of aftershave tipped over me and my erogenous zones I sat in reception sweating like a blind lesbian in a fish shop! Gradually the lads all began to arrive one by one again meaning Yecora was horrendously late, they in turn ruffled my hair and gave that annoying whey hey chant that gets on your 'Threpney's'. They were ready for boarding the night bus when I decided to wait outside away from the increasing raucousness. At approximately ten seventeen Yecora arrived looking hassled and was again apologising for her lateness, I didn't mind at all, her smile erased any negative thoughts and it understood the difficulties when foreign cultures work later than us Brits because they have siestas mid afternoon and return to work as we are heading home for the day, it wasn't easy to tell exactly when you would finish. Anyway the main thing was that she had arrived and with air conditioning in her sister in law's Cherokee jeep, whey hey!

The meal was excellent and so was the restaurant, it had traditional Mexican bandits as waiters and music to match, but the food was the best I'd ever tasted. This was a holiday I surely wouldn't forget. Not only was I beginning to fall in love but been treated to sights and places we wouldn't have even known about if I wasn't for 18/08/00. With this special number in mind I decide to tell Yecora about my superstition and the story with my lucky gold chain.

I had for the previous few years insisted in travelling with the chain as a lucky charm, even if I didn't wear it, it became an essential item which brought me good luck. I knew we would meet again in England but decided the day before that I would give the chain to Yecora that evening as a promise to meet again so she could return it, she was bowled over with this gesture and I could see tears welling up in her eyes, she knew this was the beginning and not the end. I think my actual words were "I'll come back for you", smooth eh? Cue Sade 'Smooth operator'.

Yecora handed me a ring from her finger and we agreed to exchange when we next saw each other, she also pulled an envelope out of her handbag and said this was a card for me to open on the plane or when I returned home, so we both left with something from each other, which was nice. We drove back to my hotel and I tried all the radio stations for something to listen to and the one and only channel that was working played Robert Marley and the Wailers 'No Women no cry', never a bad track for one to tap one's foot to plus it defined that moment particularly well. We parked the car, embraced and shared a long loving kiss and just as I was about to close the car door I turned and instinctively said "I think I love you".

Chapter 3

It's Grim up North

I opened my envelope alone in my room before Jim and Harry returned from their last night out in Mexico, it was a card depicting the Kiss by Gustav Klimt and on the reverse there was a special note. The note said exactly what I had been feeling also, the realisation that we had something special and that we should definitely remain in close contact, it was a beautiful message and ended with hugs and kisses, I was pleased as punch.

Early the next morning we packed our bags and set off for another ten hour flight without a cigarette and the possibility of more VTB. The journey home for me was much quicker; apart from the head wind advantage the other added bonus was reading my note and tapping the ring on my little finger against anything that could make a sound. This began to wear thin on the rest of the gang, especially after ten hours cooped up like animals with no escape, still we had fun even though all everyone wanted to do was get home, have a real cup of tea, visit your own toilet and then curl up in your own bed, after six or seven fags that is.

Nigel spend most of the flight totting up scores and handing out made up awards for certain accomplishments like the biggest marlin landed [or the only one], worst sunburn, biggest woman, most money spent, least money spent and of course a special award for holiday romance. We knew it was all bachelor type childish antics but if you can't have a bit of fun then what's the point? Although I had stressed to everyone that this was no flash in the pan romance and it was the real thing, the others just teased me and I was happy to just be on the awards list and happy in my thoughts about Yecora.

We landed back in Manchester at eight in the morning after

being shunted forward six hours by the time difference. Most of us had not only this day off work but also the following day to sleep off any two week hangovers and jet lag, unfortunately for Baz he was due at work right away and promptly switched on his mobile phone which began to ring and bleep like a thing that rings and bleeps quite a lot. We did feel sorry for him but still made the mini bus journey home hell for him with endless bragging of anticipated relaxation. By eleven o'clock we had all reached our homes and begun to open piles of bills and junk mail whilst Barry was tying his tie and beginning a day's work.

Once refreshed from five hours sleep and being woken by the rumble of an empty stomach it was time visit Mum and Dad to catch up on news and for a slap up meal no doubt. It feels great to have a nice shower and put on fresh clothes after two weeks of having a sand filled crotch and wearing sweaty creased clothes. When I got to my parent's house it was a real comfort, the kind were you are so happy and relaxed with your surroundings, everything in its place, I was lucky because my parents live only two minutes away in a lovely seven bedroom Edwardian house set in private land and apart from having my independence in my little terraced house around the corner, it was still nice to hang out in the comfort at Mum and Dads.

As luck would have it my brother Pete and his family were visiting from York and my sister Ann and her family who live two more minutes away in the opposite direction were also visiting, so a house full and lots of laughs in stall, not to mention a superb diner cooked by my Mum was already being prepared on the Aga. It's funny because whenever Pete visits, my Mum always bakes apple pies and believe me when I smelt that delicious smell deriving from the flue pipe, Fajitas and guacamole were shoved to one side, at least for now anyway.

I waltzed into the kitchen through the open rear door to see everyone having a glass of wine and making those silly family jokes that haven't changed for twenty years, all this was a perfect return to home comforts, but I didn't just have a glorious tan to show for my holiday, I also had some fabulous news to tell.

I tucked into a familiar feast of food and briefly told about my holiday tails, I told about some of the stories and obviously about Yecora. I said I had met a girl and she was going to be visiting England in a couple of months and that we were serious enough to meet up again and see were it takes us. All the family made that usual whey hey sound demonstrating that they approved but were going to tease me over it every opportunity they could.

I explained the whole story to them about meeting Yecora and how we both felt about each other and I could see they were understanding that I was so excited about this change that had come about, they also laughed at my friends stories of Mexico, after all my family have known my friends since we were all kids, they understood that we all had the best holiday in an exotic unknown destination, well unknown to them until now.

One full day of doing absolutely nothing but watching sports was all the preparation I needed for the following day at work; my liver also thanked me for a well earned break from the battering it had been subjected to, not to mention my 'cutter'. My rear end had completely packed in from the amount of spicy food mixed with ridiculous amounts of alcohol. It was nothing short of a miracle that none of the gang had any incidents resulting in a journey back to the hotel donning a borrowed towel around ones waste.

The main thing that spurred me on was that there were only two days left at work and it would be weekend again, I was however itching to get on the computer and write an email to Yecora as promised. This was the year two thousand and computers were still a continued strong force in the work place following the disappointment of the Millennium bug, I really did wish for the bug to be a reality at the time just to see the blind panic it would have provoked.

Our company, like many others at that time employed a Millennium bug engineer who spent eighteen months prior preparing for the worst, on the second of January his desk had gone, poor sod. Like most of the Millennium it was nothing short of a complete let down. Anyway we had all been trained in our office to use complicated engineering estimation programmes and we were all very proficient in the fine workings of a PC, email however had only been around a short time including Manchester and I certainly didn't have my own address at that stage other than the company one. Yecora and I had switched business cards with our email addresses on and I said I would send her an email as soon as I was back at work, I'm not sure though if I had told her that I would only be arriving at work until Thursday.

Yecora was a fully trained lawyer and was working as a sub chief of the immigration department in Cancun and she seemed to be doing very well at it as well as enjoying her job at the same time, which is quite a rarity. Once I had begrudgingly hauled my frame across two cities and arrived at work I was eager to send an email.

After the first ten minutes of light banter with my colleagues about the holiday and my news about Yecora [they also couldn't pronounce her name correctly, especially with a Manc' accent] I settled into getting back up to speed with the job. Before I could ask about the news of redundancies my dad had told me about I sensed that some changes were afoot. Our manager arrived soon after and swiftly called me into his office. "Oh shit" I thought that's me pumped on my first day back.

He calmly explained the company's position and that the Manchester office was closing gradually and to have Birmingham office cover all up to Edinburgh to make way for the streamlined new look. I was to be one of many casualties from our office but the only one in our team, I was gutted but had to go with the unwritten law of last in, first out. It was not a nice feeling when someone actually says that you are being made redundant, it just sounds like you've done something wrong when you haven't.

The company were however brilliant with they way they saw me through finding another job, again they had made a specific position for someone to carry out that role as the whole place would eventually fold, I think it was the Millennium bug guys desk that they reused and just changed the pot plant and blinds.

When I had my scheduled back operation to correct a damaged disc two years previously the company had been truly great to me then also so I had no real complaints about what had happened it was just unsettling. I did later in the morning get chance to go online and to my complete astonishment there was an email waiting to be opened from Yecora, my palms became instantly like wet sponges, I was WLF.

I opened the mail and I read how she missed me already and that she hoped I had arrived home safely but she teased me about not sending her a mail before, it really lifted me to hear from her and it was just the tonic I needed, I knew everything would work out somehow. I sent a loving message back and printed the email and read it over and over all the way home as I waited to explain to my parents that I now had no job as well as no car, but I had a Mexican girlfriend all the same, well not officially, not in the classical sense.

The days and weeks passed slowly as the winter kicked in, we exchanged emails everyday and I even purchased a cheap rate phone line account so we could speak to each other on the telephone a couple of times a week also. It wouldn't be long until Yecora would be coming to London and we could eventually see each other again, I just couldn't wait, the feeling was so intense I knew that I did love her and it was the most powerful emotion I had ever experienced.

I took my little collection of emails to the quiz night and briefly read some lines to the guys, not only to brag about my romance but to reconfirm that this was not just any romance. We tittered as I read the slight spelling mistakes out, which I know is cruel but it was sweeter than anything, most of the guys knew Yecora and also described her as such a sweet girl so we just had a bit of fun with it, plus I liked the attention it attracted. Yecora's English was superb, a thousand times better than my Spanish but every forty words or so there would be a funny mistake, just as an example "I was in a bad mood" would read "I was in a bad mud" and so on and so on.

One day at work I was told I had been successful in a previous interview that I had had and could start work as soon as my redundancy period had finished; things were looking up like I knew they would. I had a nice redundancy payment due which was approximately two months pay; I had a new job with more money and a company car thrown in!

The job was still in Manchester so I would have to commute but who cared I was feeling on top of the world. It's funny though how when you come into some money yet still manage to be poor, it never seems to be enough, still. Instead of borrowing the magical three hundred pounds from someone every month it had now dropped to around two hundred, I was positively rich. After paying off all my borrowed holiday spending money and paying my initial phone bill, all the spare money had again dried up, but at least I had a shiny new car that was essentially free.

The new job went well and I fitted in quickly to the team, the only unfortunate thing was that the company was waiting for new premises to be built as they had grown so much in a short space of time and it just so happened that our team's office was situated in a converted roof space. Apart from staring at a computer screen all day and overhearing just about everyone else's phone calls there was no way of escape, a brief walk around the block at lunch time was the only view of the world during the working day. The office did have two skylights but they pointed directly upwards and as the roof touched your head when you stood up it didn't provide any view of anything of any offering. I still enjoyed it all the same and I looked forward to opening new emails from Yecora telling me of her up and coming visit, I really couldn't wait now and it was becoming a mild frustration.

The dark winter weather had arrived and so when I left the house in the morning it was dark, I spent all day in a roof space and then drove home, also in the dark. What I needed was to see the girl who had totally changed my life and then everything else would seem insignificant, it is hard work for any long distance relationship to be successful, being on the phone for forty minutes at a time and endless emails is great to be in touch but it's not the same as seeing the one you love in person and being able to see them up close.

I also had a selection of great photos from the holiday, I had printed two copies of the few I had of Yecora so I could cut some of them down to size and slip them in my wallet so I could have a 'Butchers' at them during the day, how sad is that? I know this all sounds a bit heavy but what can I say, I was head over heels in love and these little things just made it all the more wonderful. I hadn't turned soppy or anything I made sure we both had a reality check from time to time and we enjoyed making jokes about the whole thing, I would make her laugh all the time and the relationship was a healthy normal one not some weird obsessed delusion.

Finally the time had come to meet with Yecora in London, she had got a cheap flight via her work connections and was first to fly to Milan then onto London. She was scheduled to spend her two weeks with her old school friend Maria and her partner Alberto who was Italian and their son Miguel. They lived in Islington and although Yecora's Mother and family thought she was going to stay with them all the time, we had made loose plans for Yecora to come and visit the north of England and obviously stay at my house, alone, with me, in my bed. This would have been construed as fifty seventh base I expect, but no one needed to know only us and Maria, and my family and friends and the people at work, oh and the quiz master.

Yecora has three elder brothers and I would expect she hadn't told them that she was about to spend time alone with some English guy she had only known for a couple of months, but Yecora knew herself what type of person I was and that she was completely safe in my company. Yecora's Father sadly past away when she was three years old and I could imagine that she would have kept it a secret from him also, for the time being at least. Apparently Yecora's Father when he was younger was a very successful American Football player; he starred for the University team in Mexico City and was particularly famous in the fifties and sixties.

He played in front of around ten thousand people regularly and was a feared opponent going by the nick name of 'Loco Lecanda' as in Crazy Lecanda, Lecanda obviously being the family surname. He was in his early forties when he died of a heart attack whilst playing Fronton a type of squash, something which you just can't imagine when leaving four young children and a wife behind, so sad. It was her father who named her Yecora after he had been working as a Civil Engineer in the Sierra Madre Mountains in the north of Mexico. He came across a small picturesque village named Santana de Yecora and returned home with stories of the beauty and magic it afforded him, soon after Yecora the girl was born.

Although I wasn't applying any pressure on Yecora to meet her at the airport I did however want to see her as soon as was humanly possible. We agreed I could meet her at Maria's house soon after she arrived and spend a couple of hours with her catching up from where we had left off. It was a Tuesday when she arrived, late afternoon, early evening so my plan was to drive straight from work from in Manchester at five pm to my Sister Helen's house which was south London. I expected I would arrive around eight o'clock at Helen's house and then I would call Maria to see if Yecora had arrived.

As I journeyed to London I made a call to se if Yecora had in fact arrived and I introduced myself to Maria of course, she sounded very easy going and made me feel a lot more at ease about the whole visit, it was after all quite nerve racking. I didn't have any serious doubts just the normal ones that enter your head, what if she's changed her mind, what if she's had a change of heart, maybe she's lost interest in the whole relationship, anyway Maria said Yecora couldn't wait to see me and she was making her way across London as we spoke. She reported that Yecora had had some delay in Milan and that all her luggage had been temporarily lost, not a good start, plus finding your way across London at night is also a pretty stressful experience even for a local.

I arrived at my sister's house and discussed my plan which was to go back the way I had just come across London to the North, see Yecora, return once more to Helen's, get a few hours sleep and go straight to Manchester at three thirty in the morning, simple. I made my way to Maria's house and went around in circles through the one way systems of London and eventually parked outside her house just before ten o'clock, exhausted. This would be a quick and possibly a desperate sounding visit but nevertheless I just could not wait to see her.

I knocked on the door and waited, Maria answered the door and in my appalling Spanish I happened to mention reference to Brazilian casserole once again. Maria said Yecora had just arrived and she was just powdering her conk, I got the impression she was doing what all girls do and making sure she was looking her best, especially after travelling for a whole day. So I made my way inside and sat at the kitchen table with Maria and her family, they were really so nice and we hit it off straight away, it's nice when that happens, when you meet normal people without attitude who you can actually have great conversation with and feel completely comfortable with. Alberto didn't take long to switch the conversation to football and to Preston North End football club, he even knew who Tom Finney was, we would get along just fine I thought. It also made the intense wait to see Yecora that bit easier.

It seemed to take forever for Yecora to appear, with my overactive imagination I couldn't help picturing her squeezing through the bathroom window and making a nervous escape or more simply just squeezing one out after a long journey. I really shouldn't have pickled my brain as a teenager with our Special Brew and Cider parties, the affects were haunting me.

Finally Yecora slowly eased herself around the kitchen door exposing her unforgettable smile. Wow I thought, I was right, she was amazingly stunning, my smile then began to challenge hers and before I knew it she was sat on my knee and we talked as if we had been friends forever, the magic was undoubtedly still there for all to see. We discussed many subjects in our small group and as the Spanish speakers conversed I found myself stealing sneaky glimpses of what could have been the appearance an angel in my presence. She was every bit what I had remembered, I was so happy I had almost forgotten I had to be up and on the road to work in just four hours so we hugged and kissed, which was nice and agreed to talk tomorrow once she had settled in and found her bags of course.

I then did something appalling which I would like to remain a secret but Yecora would be the first to let the Iguana out of the bag, I had made a music tape for her! I know, what a dick head, I just don't know what came over me; if I listened to it now I think I would vomit. It was so unlike me but at the time it made sense and I ashamedly imagine Yecora retreating to the kitchen and saying in Spanish "The knob head has done me a tape" anyway enough said about that the better. I deliriously made the journey back across London and told my sister about my romantic adventure then retired to bed.

Once at my desk the following morning not even the excitement of the oncoming weekend could keep me awake. In the stuffy loft space, tapping away on the computer, adding up figures and speaking to suppliers on the phone with a sluggish voice I literally could have curled up under the desk and snoozed for the rest of the day amid the hustle and bustle of the office.

Finally by six thirty I collapsed on the sofa in my own little house. I called Yecora at Maria's house as agreed and listened as she told me of her encounters in the busy capital, her bags had arrived so finally she could change her smeeds or grundigs to those who don't know what smeeds are. The conversation was around ten minutes long, thirty less than normal because we were both on the same soil we felt much closer, less lost if you like. This came as a welcome relief to us both and we felt more like a real couple, it's strange to describe but we were happy and content with our lot.

The rest of the week moved quite quickly and each day I was filled in with the latest news on what she had done, where she had visited and how she longed to see me. I had managed to wangle the following Monday off work so the plan was for me to travel to London from work on the Friday, see Yecora and her friends [now mine also as we found out very quickly] I would sleep at Helen and Gary's house because after all we should be proper about these things shouldn't we? There would be plenty of time for visiting double figure bases over the next few days.

I arrived in London at Maria's house around nine o'clock and Yecora was all ready and waiting, I could see she was absolutely delighted to see me, we had a life saving hug and kiss then set out for the nearby wine bar to talk and have some real time together. Maria and Alberto watched and smiled as we walked hand in hand down the street and I knew myself from then on everything would be fine, it was all to be as I had imagined, strangely.

As we talked and drank wine I remembered that Yecora was not the world's best drinker, not like us filthy Brits who abuse the right to a casual drink. We did however have a most wonderful evening, it not only broke the ice that little bit further but we felt that the whole bar was looking at this beautiful couple so in love, we looked pretty good together I can tell you. It finally came to a stage where we felt on top of the world and the time alone did us both a mountain of good. Two glasses of red wine later and I could see Yecora's eyes glistening so I walked her home gave her a loving kiss and raced back to my sister's house in preparation for our next big milestone.

Before long I once again circumnavigated London and arrived back in Islington on the Saturday morning, Yecora was on time and ready with a small case packed in preparation to be carried off into the North of England with a complete stranger, just kidding of course. We had coffee with Alberto and Maria and I could still sense their excitement too, they believed in the relationship even though it was incredibly young and still the question of 'asking her out' as we call it in England or used to, still hadn't dawned on numb nuts here. We set off on our journey north and before long we were at ease once again with each others company, it was just so special I find it hard to put into words.

How can two people from different corners of the globe, with very little time physically together be getting along so well? I felt like I was being carried away by a magical spell and forgive me for actually saying this but I thought I was in heaven. Yecora gently fingered my neck hairs as I drove [sorry, I'm just picturing a selection of my friends reading that aloud] which was another reason to feel secure in the situation we were in. We were both gradually finding out more and more about each others personalities and amazingly we were of ideal compatibility, she like egg and chips, I liked egg and chips etc. One of the only things that we didn't have in common was that

I can hold my bladder for more than fifteen minutes where as Yecora needed a waz with every gear change.

We had a great weekend planned, it involved visiting the jewel of the north, no not Knott End but the Lake District. I feel so proud of the fact that one of the most stunning areas of England is right on our doorstep and I didn't want to waste any time in showing her a few sights, including my most favourite drinking establishment in the whole world. It's called the Hole in the Wall in Bowness, I don't know why but it holds a little magic for me that place. It is over four hundred years old and mostly built from local slate and usually has a travelling folk singer strumming away in the beer garden, the beer is top notch and the prawn sandwiches always give me a bonk on!

After umpteen piss stops we eventually arrived in gloomy Preston, it really was grim up north. I adopted the posh route in from the motorway. It was something I had planned in my own mind previously but not long before, Ray another of the gang had told me that he had done the same with his international girlfriend. Both myself and Ray had met girls abroad and become very seriously involved, the only difference was that he had met his girlfriend on a gay love boat in Amsterdam, slightly different to my story but as romantic nonetheless.

Three months previous to the Mexico trip twenty of the gang had travelled to Amsterdam for a weekend stag party; I had purposely acted as a work chauffeur the week before and driven a group of company executives to watch rugby in London to earn the extra cash so I could make the trip. It was pretty hard going as I earned my one hundred and eighty pounds cash to drive a hired mini bus from six am starting in Preston then to Leeds where our business development manger lived who was in charge of the big event.

I even had to bribe our young office junior so I could be the driver instead of him, I had begun a habit of not wanting to miss out on anything and even though our company bosses were going to be present I was still prepared to do the task. I arrived at his house right on time, we loaded all the corporate drinks, snacks, cutlery, plates, cups and saucers all neatly as he had intended. Jeff was his name and he contentedly nestled into the front seat besides me as we rotated around his quiet street to set on our way, unfortunately as we reached half way around the u-turn the carefully arranged tea set decided to go for an early morning stroll along with the hob knobs.

I think we or I had woken about a dozen families from their sleep in a manoeuvre that even Michael Schumacher would have been proud of, even so Jeff being a happy sole pissed himself laughing to my wonderment and we sped off to the next pick up point. The whole journey encompassed Leeds then Manchester, Liverpool, Leicester then London and the same in reverse following the rugby match. That was a long day I can tell you, I had a super time though mixing with company big wigs, they befriended me enough to insist that I came with them at each of their points of interest, luckily I sensibly had only two pints of Guinness all day, un-sensibly I had forgotten to eat anything.

The journey home was horrendous, following the first happy hour every one had become to drunk and irritable, by the time we reached Liverpool one of party had managed to decorate the rear of the bus with previously digested foodstuff, the bus had become a crime scene. All I recall from there on is physically slapping myself in the face with all the windows opened and the stereo on full blast just to try and stay awake, it was three o'clock in the morning before I finally took the junction to Preston via the cats eyes for guidance, it was the hardest money I had ever earned but worth every penny.

The Amsterdam trip was doomed from the start, we arrived having lost one guy to a Dutch prison, he had arrived alone a few hours before the main group and not only managed to lose his passport but also his ability to speak, walk or talk and was promptly arrested by an early afternoon bobby. The rest of us trudged through the airport then the train station and towards the hotel, we grouped in reception to be told that the best man had mistakenly booked the trip for the following month and the place was fully booked this particular weekend.

The upshot was that we were guided to a travel information office that luckily found us all a hotel for the weekend, the only draw back or maybe not in this case was that we had been booked into a hotel boat on the dark dock of Amsterdam port. This boat as it so happened was run by two gentlemen with impressive moustaches who tended to walk funny and have lots of their male friends visit and look decidedly dodgy all together. Anyway the weekend turned out to be an absolute blast, we had so much fun it was unreal, we just didn't get much sleep that was all, as we all tried to keep one eye on your cabin door, as it were. So anyway, Ray had met Nicola from Canada along the way and he also formed a firm long distance relationship which then also in turn led to becoming something much more.

I helped Yecora into my house with her bags and made her feel as comfortable as I could. We watched some TV and drank tea, then we smooched for a while on the sofa and before long it was time to go to bed. This obviously was going to be a bit awkward for Yecora; I knew we wouldn't be having sex together, not just yet anyway. I knew that a long time ago and as we had only just been reunited I didn't want to push her into something she was uncomfortable with. We retired to the bedroom and as I returned from brushing my teeth I gazed around the room to find where Yecora was, I suddenly spotted movement and she had found a dark corner behind the bed to squat and change into her pyjamas, I didn't know they still made them.

It was so sweet; she looked like a little mouse scrating in the corner of the room. I hadn't seen pyjamas since I was a kid and found it a little bit strange to see but then again who was the strange one hear? I hadn't worn anything in bed for the last fifteen years so tonight with my boxer shorts on I felt over dressed. I realised quickly that it was most probable that Yecora was in fact a virgin, here in England that would sound strange at her age of twenty six but the Latin way of life is so different and in my mind much more saintly or pure. I thought it was wonderful, I know that every guy in the world would jump at the chance of getting his leg over but in some special cases it pays more dividends to be patient. I had begun what I thought was another side of our relationship that was pure and realised that this was unique for this day and age, I was to become celibate for the foreseeable future, are you having that one?

We cuddled up to each other in bed and slept like two love birds in a nest, it was glorious and a refreshing change to be the way we were. We woke early, changed and paid a visit to my Parents house before setting off to see the beautiful Lake District, it wasn't ideal conditions as the sky was grey and full of clouds plus it was freezing cold, approximately two degrees Celsius and thirty less than she was used to. There is always something quite romantic about walking in the brisk cold winter with woolly jumpers and holding the hand of your girlfriend, it was cosy. We went to my parents and I was always proud to introduce them and show off their impressive house, Yecora was impressed by it all and she also got along with my mum and dad right from the word go. Mum got out the best china and Rich tea biscuits and inevitably the conversation turned to my childhood and out came the photos. I could only stand thirty minutes of this coupled with my dad's jokes so we swigged our tea and headed north.

By now the cold was beginning to get to Yecora, she had about four layers on and I suspect her pyjamas were under their somewhere. We had a great day visiting some lovely scenic views of the lakes; we then arranged to meet with Nick who happened to be in the area conducting business. We met in the grand Old England Hotel in Windermere and Nick was amazed at the blueness of Yecora's mouth and lips, she was beginning to literally freeze. We had fun discussing the holiday and reminiscing over good times had by all, on our way back home Yecora giggled wildly at spotting that Nick had one blue sock on and one black one, it did seem funny at the time because he was suited for work and when he sat down this glorious blue sock was fully exposed. It was very dark in the winter mornings after all.

We stopped for evening dinner on the way home in a lovely warm, typical English countryside restaurant and we gazed at each over a candle lit table festooned with the local cuisine but done tastefully, not just heated slop as with most places you find these days.

The next day we ventured to the metropolis of Manchester and walked the retail gangplank, girls love that kind of thing, for me it's similar to tortures found in and around China and I would rather have all my teeth removed than wander pointlessly from shop to shop then back again. My plastic just about stood the damage but truthfully I actually enjoyed the whole experience for once, accompanied by my Latin non-lover.

All too soon we were heading for London again, it was Monday and we spent the day visiting some cool places chosen by our friends and guides. On our way to London we took a detour to visit my sister, I called her mobile phone and she was having lunch with her boyfriend Gary and some friends just outside London so we arranged to glide past and make a formal introduction. We walked into the restaurant to find them all pissed as farts, we attempted to blend in best we could sipping a glass of wine and nodding politely.

Not many questions or conversation was directed at Yecora, this was probably a good thing as Yecora was a little bit shy and embarrassed any way plus it's never a good time to meet someone when they've been on a 'Leo Sayer'. It's just impossible to get up to speed with people with four hours head start. After an hour of listening to others having a great time we eventually made a move, we gave the group a lift home, shook hands, kissed and waved them goodbye and headed to meet Maria and Alberto.

We arrived at Maria's house and promptly set out to do some sightseeing with them around London. After a while we paired off into couples and Yecora and I walked along the River Thames embankment occasionally stopping to kiss and take in the early evening light show of London's impressive architecture.

It was then that Yecora took me by surprise, she obviously had something she wanted to say for some time and it was now or never for her as we had little or no time alone. First of all she wanted to clarify the status of our relationship and being slightly naïve to the old fashioned Latin way I had neglected to actually say to her "Will you be my girlfriend". Once it was out in the open I felt a certain joy at having to ask the question, it gave the whole situation a wonderful feeling of cleanliness and morality. I asked the question with a beaming smile and her reply of "Yes of course" was matched with a knock out smile of her own. The second of Yecora's worries was a little more serious and difficult for her to get off her chest; it was the subject of sex.

Now don't get me wrong, I had thought about it a lot myself and because I was so attracted to her it was only natural that I would want to get closer and make love, I hate that saying by the way. Yecora explained how from the age of a small girl she had wished to meet the right man to settle down with and marry and only then would she and her faith allow a roll in the hay. I replied I am also a Catholic and delighted in the many ways of our faith, it seemed so beautiful the way we stood there, hands held tightly discussing something that was so special to her and her eventual husband, whoever that may be. We did not know what the future held for us both and more so as we were venturing into a four and a half thousand mile long distance relationship and I assured her that I found her reasons and beliefs truly amazing, inspiring and down right admirable.

It helped Yecora so much after that discussion because she had finally told me of her situation plus I had assured her of my willy support, sorry willing support. It meant that there would be no pressure to head in that direction and not at this stage anyway to have added pressure to discuss marriage just for the sake of hot, passionate lustfulness. Heavy petting however was the new way forward; we would have been ejected from every swimming baths in the land, had we gone that is.

We strolled for a couple more hours knowing we had very little one on one time left together so we soaked up every second we had together. We were blissfully in love and no matter what obstacles came in our way we could and would get through it somehow. We didn't want to think to much about the future, about how this would end, we just felt sure that if we had each other then someway we would again just follow the signs and be guided to our fate, whatever that had install.

Later that evening we prepared to say our goodbyes once again, this wasn't going to be an easy ride by any stretch of the imagination, the next few months would be just as hard if not harder than the previous ones. We discussed plans for me to visit Yecora for a Christmas break perhaps, only two and a half months away, it sounds like a lifetime when you cradle the one you love and say your farewells but on paper ten weeks can pass in the blink of an eye. We both had realised this would be a situation we would become very familiar with and both of us had to come up with ways to deal with it. Ever the optimist I called upon strength in the knowledge that Yecora's smile would always be there to greet me wherever and whenever we would next meet. After all we still had technology on our side and by now digital technology was taking over; we had video, photos and telephone so we would never be any more than a flick of a switch away.

Following a lengthy goodbye I made my umpteenth journey across London to back to Helen's house for a well earned sleep before yet another trek north, directly to my desk at work.

The next few weeks were spent scouring the internet for cheap flights at Christmas time to Mexico, not any easy task especially when my money had completely dried up and I was reliant each month on family and friends to bail me out. Maybe I was doing something wrong; everybody else seemed to be managing quite well, especially the bachelors, that's just life I suppose.

One good piece of news though came in the form of taking a lodger into my home, this was not just any lodger though, it was my old mate Bazza. He had been renting elsewhere and his contract was to expire from the New Year and we came up with the plan to live together, not only would I have much needed additional income but we would have a complete ball, it would be like living in a party bubble and even a quiet night in would end in tears of laughter, I couldn't wait. For the time being I had to struggle on and missing Yecora was really all I could think about. We did write handwritten letters to each other as well as emails, it was always nice to go to the post office and collect something all the way from across the Atlantic Ocean and it never failed to brighten up my spirits.

My job was going really well in the whole apart from I

always felt that a brick wall was there to meet me at the project end, I guess I was stuck in a rut and would have to just keep turning up to work and see what the day had to offer. There were always plenty of companies in Preston that I could approach thus saving on travel expenses, for now though I put the idea to the back of my mind and decided to soldier on regardless and pressed on with finding myself a flight.

Chapter 4

It's a Miracle!

The trip was all set, I was to fly direct again from Manchester during Christmas week and Yecora had arranged for me to stay in her friends house for the week I was there, her friends apparently were also having a vacation somewhere or another. I managed to find a reasonable price for the flight but during any holiday period you can expect to pay over the odds, which I did. The time eventually came to leave and I said goodbye to family and friends and I could sense that they all supported me and my actions entirely, they were even visibly a little bit excited too about my Mexican adventure.

I had only booked for one week as I had to get back to work straight after the Christmas holidays, the second day of the New Year in fact. I would at least have a nice sun tan for the New Year parties and still be able to sample my Mother's wonderful festive cooking.

The flight this time, alone, was long and I mean long. There were also pockets of VTB to contend with whilst cramped next to a complete stranger wanting to know your life story just as you are about to doze off, finally. It was a nightmare and I couldn't help thinking that when I have to do this next time I'm going to take out a loan and travel first class, the trouble with that is though, first class is almost identical on this kind of flight, the major difference for the extra premium was a tatty old curtain divide that looks like it had shrunk in the wash.

I was really excited about seeing Yecora and all the added extras that I hadn't taken in on the last trip. The last trip we were mainly confined to our resort and it would be nice to witness and sample more of the real Mexico as opposed to the rich hotel zone, I'm not insinuating that the rest of the city is poor, just that the hotel zone is governed by an unbelievable high volume of tourism and the money that goes with it. I wanted to see more of the magical Mexican life.

Once through the arduous and sweaty customs escapade I realised that the sun in Mexico never really has a winter break, it was sweltering hot and humid but the funny thing was I was seeing Mexican locals with pullovers on, for them it was winter at 26 degrees! As I worked my way through the lines of tourist I wondered also about Yecora's family, if they would accept me or what their thoughts and fears were about this pale faced English man with a funny accent. All I knew was that somehow I would manage to pull it off, after all no one could ever doubt that Yecora and I were in love, so why should I get all WLF?

It was December 24th, Christmas eve to me and Christmas day in Latin America, I know, news to me also. Apparently the exact moment to celebrate Christmas is midnight between the two days as Jesus was supposedly born, so I guess both days are correct in one way, the only thing was that I was used to it the European way.

Yecora was already at the airport to greet me and it was a delight just to see her, it made all the waiting seem worth while. She had borrowed her eldest Brother Hugo's car which was a VW Beetle, the new shape, which was nice, particularly as it had AC. She told me that we were having traditional Christmas dinner at her uncle's house later in the evening so it would make sense to go direct to my place of abode to get changed and meet all the family later at the meal. I wasn't nervous at all, just excited and intrigued as to what a Mexican Christmas entailed.

We arrived at where I was to stay downtown, this was much more like the real Mexico I had envisaged and soaked up all the culture presented before me. The house was lovely and comfortable, it was beautifully decorated and well arranged and perfect for my needs. Yecora and I shared another spine tingling kiss and said a brief adios until I was to be picked up in three hours for the family dinner.

I took a shower and lazed in front of the TV to unwind from the long flight; I took regular cigarette breaks in the garden and smiled politely at the neighbours. After a short while I wondered why the house was full of pictures and ornaments depicting cherubs and things of a female touch, this was supposed to be a guy's house and his friend shared with him. It wasn't until I saw a framed picture of two Chihuahua puppies wearing little pink tank tops that the penny dropped, I was in the house of two gay men and suddenly had a flash back to my Amsterdam accommodation.

Not that there is anything wrong with two men sharing their lives together, just I hadn't been expecting it, why didn't she just tell me? I chuckled to myself at the things my friends would have to say once I told them of my amusing story. They had already begun to poke fun at me over my Mexican romance; it was all nice things though that made the situation more fun. During our meetings at the MNC I had let it slip that I had become celibate and the reasons for it, I had never been one to kiss and tell so I explained my private and personal things about Yecora in brief, just enough information for them to make fun at me without harming Yecora's privacy at the same time.

I dressed smartly for dinner with a shirt and trousers and waited for my lift to arrive. Yecora arrived almost on time, which was nice and her middle brother Gustavo was also in the car, so we were formally introduced and we made for her uncle's house for Christmas dinner. After some five minutes of Spanish banter between Yecora and her brother, Gustavo looked over his shoulder and posed the question "So, why have you travelled all this way just to see my sister"? I replied swiftly "Because I love her". I think it shocked all three of us into silence and we continued the journey with that thought in our minds.

Suddenly my nerves were beginning to nudge further to the front and take the lead role in the proceedings, combined with abnormal sweating and damp patches appearing all over my shirt I began to shake like a shitting dog! If I could just get over the first introductions without making a fool of myself I would be ok. The three of us approached the door and with a ring of the bell the door swung open to reveal the whole family awaiting our arrival.

Our host uncle Miguel shouted loudly "It's a miracle, Yecora has a boyfriend". Well what an entrance, what an ice breaker, we all laughed out loud at Yecora's expense of course, she was visibly displaying a rouge glow from embarrassment as we pressed on inside. The house was very nice indeed and all laden with Christmas decorations, a huge tree and a beautifully arranged crib. Gradually one by one I was introduced to all the family, Yecora's Mum, aunt Lulu, two other brothers Roman and Hugo, Hugo's wife Alexandra and uncle Miguel's daughter Andrea and her husband Alexandro. Following the class entrance I had just made the introductions were a blessing, everyone was very nice to me right from the start and made me feel very much at ease which made me relax a lot more and stemmed the flow of sweat considerably.

As we sat in the lounge waiting for dinner to be served we prepared for present opening, I had given Yecora a small contribution to include me in the system that was in place, the system I think is called secret Santa. I had also purchased Yecora some presents from the UK and we exchanged our personal gifts earlier in my digs. The system was to pick a family name and buy a gift for that person and once all sat around to hand out the gift for opening, it worked a treat and everyone already had inside information on what their gift partner ideally wanted.

It was a good system and works out much cheaper than buying everyone some useless gift that they will never use or appreciate, I unfortunately had joined the list very late and walked away with a lovely decorative candle and a small motorcycle shaped clock. I made sure I was visibly enthralled with my gifts as if I had wished for them all along. During the whole process Roman had taken it upon himself to fix drinks for everyone, I knew I couldn't drink beer at the Christmas table, maybe there would be some red wine on offer. I was in the land of whiskey drinkers and although I didn't and couldn't really drink it I again made it clear that I wanted nothing else, far to polite again to speak out my real mind, I think that's the British way though, stupid I know.

Ten whiskeys later I cast my lazy eye around the room and

saw that Hugo and Alexandro were holding court with the group as the proceeding really got under way. Gustavo however had fixed an eye right upon me and as I casually turned my head pretending to look elsewhere but maintaining a 'cocked' eye I noticed he was studying me very closely. I suppose I would do exactly the same if I had a little sister who had brought a foreigner around for dinner; you would want to know how this guy works and what his real intentions are. Each time I looked back through my ever decreasing eyesight he was staring again, due to the drink I couldn't help to start to snigger nervously, you know like when in class at school and you know you shouldn't but just can't help yourself, this lead to the return of sweat marks resembling a map of Africa under each armpit.

Although I was starting to loosen up more, could I still pull off what seemed like a virtual faultless performance so far? My sniggering however was destined to let me down at the final fence; I had spotted a new occurrence that fuelled my uncontrollable internal laughter. It was an enormous centipede, a jet big black one that looked like a giant turd edging further towards Uncle Miguel's foot as he stood chatting near the fire place. Nobody but me had noticed it, probably because everyone was in deep conversation [except for Gustavo of course who was now plotting how to dispose of the body] I didn't think I could hold on any longer and began to bite my lip hard, I wondered if I should say something or just get up and beat the thing to death with my shoe, maybe it was the family pet? Oh the dilemma! Before I wet myself Uncle Miguel casually flicked the mutant insect with the side of his shoe right into the fire place and nonchalantly carried on with his conversation, he must have known it was there all along.

We moved into the dinning room and to the table which was spectacularly arranged and in a very similar way to a traditional British Christmas Dinner, which was very reassuring. The only absence was that of Brussels sprouts and a jug of gravy, apart from that we were singing from the same hymn sheet [I hate that saying but seems appropriate as we said grace] This was after all a very religious family and the conversation maintained that theme until Alex interrupted with some close to the bone smutty jokes, Hugo whispered to me

"It's ok, the mother fucker's from the north, they speak like that " Well actually it wasn't really a whisper, more of a 'I hope everyone hears me' kind of whisper. I liked Hugo, I understood his humour right from the beginning and everyone else too, they all seemed so down to earth and lots of fun, in a way very much like my family I thought as a bread roll whistled past my ear.

Yecora's Mum was also very nice, she was a very well turned out lady and had kept her looks which is always a good sign for the daughter in years to come, a good check system to imagine how your partner may look in forty years time. I was a little shocked that Hugo blatantly swore especially in front of his mother but she made me feel more comfortable as I realised it was a staged joke. She also helped me out when the Spanish got too much and translated much of the conversation particularly well as she was an English teacher.

The language was fast and furious, I made out some words but by the time I had figured it out we were three conversations away to respond. The talk changed from English to Spanish so quickly that when any questions were directed at me it was difficult to know, we would be confronted with an embarrassing silence as they awaited my response. Gradually I got the hang of it and answered during the correct allocated slots with clear and precise answers.

We talked about my career and interests, and then England and the Monarchy and even politics, not my strongest subject and I was put to shame a couple of times by their superior knowledge on my own Government. I was also quizzed on my strange accent that slipped through more and more with each glass of whisky. Being from the Northern County of Lancashire it was inevitable that some of my words would be difficult to make out, especially if you had never experienced these beautiful tones before.

What a fine mixture though across the table, Lancashire meets Latin America, it was like Fred Dibnah meets Jennifer Lopez ['am sorry love, y'all 'av to speak up] a complete misuse of the Queen's English.

The conclusion following the nights proceeding was a resounding success, I had finally meet one fifth of the family and I thought it had gone terribly well. The one thing I did come away with was with the knowledge that I was made so welcome by these lovely people and I could just relax and be myself. Even Gustavo was by now happy to release me from his watchful glare and we chatted all the way home to my gay love shack. Knowing that bit more about Yecora's family and the similarities between my family also made the trip even more enchanting, I slowly drifted off to sleep dreaming of the loveliness of the whole situation as I looked at my splendid Christmas presents through tired eyes .

My deep sleep was suddenly woken by loud Banshee like shouting right outside my window; it was early morning, bright and sunny. I jumped to my feet and all sorts of terrible things flashed through my mind, what the hell was it? It kept going, repeating the same words; I fumbled with the window blind to stare my attacker in the eye only to be met with some poor old fart on a knackered old bike selling huge barrels of water. He was still screeching an inaudible "Aqua" as he peddled off down the street with buckled wheels. That was quite some alarm clock I thought as I sparked a fag.

It was my official Christmas day now and I showered and dressed ready for going to Church with some of Yecora's family. The Church service was one of my first in a very long time indeed and it was quite enjoyable, it wasn't to long and apart from the heat I was glad I agreed to go along. There was a feeling of a fashion show about the whole thing which made me laugh, most people were to busy looking over their shoulders to gawp at who had just arrived thirty seven minutes late to really concentrate on the mass. What I didn't enjoy was the fighting in the car park to scramble to your car first to get into pole position for the exit, so road rage did exist other than just in England and these people did it in style.

As the week progressed I witnessed more and more scenes of bewilderment on the roads, I know that I was in the Caribbean and things here are a touch slower and less well organised but the driving was nothing short of shocking. Cars, buses and even Police cars all driving with their hazard lights on for absolutely no reason whatsoever, then all of a sudden the car two lanes to your right decides he should be now turning left and all hell breaks loose!

What are quite amusing though are the sights you see that you just wouldn't in England. One guy was peddling his three wheeler bike carrying a set of eight feet high ornate steel railings in his front basket and stopped besides us at the lights, which this time had been obeyed. [Whilst on the subject of traffic lights, the most annoying thing known to man has to be the way people behind you sound their horn a millisecond after the lights change to green. I mean come on, this is just ridiculous behaviour, and not something I will waste any further time or effort noting].

It wasn't uncommon to witness all sorts of house hold goods being carried on scooters and knackered old car roofs, coffee tables, gas cylinders, you name it. I had to laugh though when I saw a middle aged man and his wife [I presume it was his wife] bobbing along on a moped and he had decided it was wise for him alone to wear headgear [albeit a construction hard hat, no use at all in a road accident, even if it did stay on] whilst his poor wife, who was twice his size, frantically struggled to maintain a grip of his pants as they sped off around a sharp bend, fuck you Jack I'm alright, as the saying goes. I had begun to wonder about the state of some of the vehicles allowed to use the road, maybe their system was different to ours but if you'd seen some of these death traps flying past you carrying four times the designed amount of people dodging pot holes, it really was something quite different.

One of the massive cultural differences between England and Latin America that is plain to see is the way of greeting somebody. In England we are famous for our ability to avoid any physical contact whatsoever, we feel more comfortable with just a pleasant hand shake and a nod of the head. Whereas in Latin America they go to second base on each and every encounter throughout the day, every day.

Every woman receives a peck on the cheek and if you are not a stranger then this is combined with a hug. The men who aren't strangers give a strong hand shake which rolls into a shoulder to shoulder manly hug coupled with a pat on the back followed with a final hand shake signalling the end of the display. Now isn't that much better than the English way, not only does it show more compassion but it also gives those men struggling to meet women a chance of a visit to second base. It's funny because I love my mother more than words can say but she only receives a hug on birthdays and at Christmas, isn't that a crying shame, something should be done.

My week with Yecora however didn't involve any bumpy roads, it was all plain sailing, and we acted as if we had never been apart, as if we had always been together. We ventured out to some amazing places along the beach, into other local coastal resorts, sometimes with her friends, sometimes alone. We would however always end the night with a least an hour off watching TV at my place, where we could do what couples do and just cosy up on the sofa and be in complete bliss together. The only down side was the fact I had to leave so soon, it was almost New Year and I had to be back at my desk in literally thirty hours time.

We had had a wonderful time but had to face the truth, we didn't know when we would see each other next and we would have to resign to the fact that full telephone communication would be resumed and confirmed we'd be there in each others hour of need. It was quite sad really, it required a huge amount of commitment and although many long distance relationships would diminish from this stage onwards we vowed to keep our faith and continue to be honest and truthful. We had to start the New Year apart from each other but we certainly vowed we would be ending it all the much stronger for it, after the mountain we had to climb we would be strong enough to face anything.

It was time to say goodbye to the family and make our way to the airport, we made the journey in complete silence with only the CD player to break the noise, it played U2 and 'Stuck in a moment, you can't get out of', Bono was Yecora's hero and he summed up our mood particularly well. It was the only time that my emotions begun to get the better of me, I almost shed a tear which was not like me at all, I have always been very strong and Yecora the same. We kissed and waved goodbye and I began the dreary flight home to a grey and miserable Lancashire, at least I could still have some of my Mum's turkey sandwiches though, that was all I had to cling onto.

Chapter 5

The Ring

The plane landed at Manchester and like so many of the British most of the passengers were still dressed for sunshine weather and as we lined up to collect our luggage we must have looked a real sight to onlookers. There was burnt flesh everywhere to be seen from the good looking right to the larger framed Brit abusing the right to wear revealing clothing, at this stage I just wanted to get home and have a nice cup of tea and spark a fag.

I had left my car at the airport for convenience as I had only been away for one week and it cost the same as getting a taxi or the train so I loaded my bags into the boot and started the engine. Snow was beginning to fall and cover the ground rapidly, what a contrast to the Christmas scene I had just left in the Caribbean. With a quick time calculation I estimated it was almost one o'clock in the morning of the New Year in Mexico. With another calculation of the cost of a mobile to mobile call I rang Yecora to wish her Happy New Year, after all I wanted to be the first to say it to her and remain in her thoughts as she celebrated a new start for us both.

The line rang as I sat in my car waiting to hear her lovely sweet voice, after a few rings she answered. I can't tell you the value of that call and what t meant to us both; all I can say is that I drove home with the biggest smile which erased any doubt that had crept in during the previous ten hour flight. Yecora was absolutely knocked out when she heard my voice, she almost cried herself, her friends around her cheered and that I think made her feel so much happier with our gloomy situation, everything was going to be alright.

The next day at work was pretty much the same as where I had left it; I had quickly and wisely come to terms with my new situation which included the fact that my undercarriage was collecting dust. There wasn't much we could do about any of it, just to continue in our belief that everything would work out somehow.

January soon vanished and it was rapidly nearing March. Another summer trip to Mexico for the boys was being banded around, lead by me of course. Baz had finally completed his rental commitment and now had moved in with me, we straight away had so much fun, like being two school boys allowed to live in an adult's world. Barry put up with many late night phone calls from me to Mexico and had to endure the sound of me explaining my daily trials and tribulations not to mention the 'You hang up first' ritual.

During one of our phone calls I mentioned to Yecora that there was a Mexican film on TV tomorrow night called 'Like water for chocolate' she knew the film very well and told me how that it was a very famous movie which everyone back home had seen. The story line depicted the old Mexico and virtues of days gone by, she told me not to take it too seriously as it was a little bit heavy in parts, well I had to watch it now didn't I and give her my opinion, and Barry's of course.

The following night Baz and I settled down to watch the film, we had been in really good spirits since he moved in and enjoyed our silly hour which was usually between ten and eleven pm. I don't know why but we always ended up crying laughing at something stupid we had seen or heard on TV or more often than not just something we had had a discussion about. It was quite normal for us to have a drink of beer or wine during an evening following a slap up student meal, neither of us really wanted cook so it was generally a take away or something on toast.

As I had mentioned, I was not the richest person around, I always had some big bill to pay around the corner and had been struggling to fill my car with petrol on a regular basis for work. I had been using so much fuel I was beginning to wonder if I should move to a job closer to home and save the money I used on fuel. I had become used to paying for petrol with my cheque book and once I'd returned to my car and driven away I always had a sense of guilt, would the cheque clear or would it not?, that was the question. One night on the way home from work in Manchester I noticed the fuel gauge was lower than zero so I coasted into a garage and because I was paying so much attention to the cheque I was going to submit I neglected to select the correct type of fuel.

One mile down the motorway the car juddered to a halt, it was the engine rejecting the diesel. I had to call Nick and my brother in law Rob to come and tow me all the way home so not even did I have to pay one hundred pounds to get it fixed but another tank of fuel was needed. So you see how these things can escalate from month to month and leave you with absolutely no spare cash at all, there was always something. Even now that Baz was paying his way I still managed not to manage, I longed for the day when I could be financially stable. There would be not much chance of that though having a girlfriend half way around the world, oh well I'll just have to go back on the bins I thought.

The movie got under way and the protagonist's characters were very interesting and it wasn't long before we both really got into the film. Baz indicated that one the girls had a fine bosom and that he would like nothing more than to offer to wash them for her, we were already into silly hour by now. Silly hour could entail anything that you could imagine; God only knows what the neighbours must of thought the night that we held our first whistling competition. We timed each other to whistle the 'Jolly Rodger' theme and it became very competitive at one stage until both our mouths were aching so much we called it a draw. I remember telling my brother Pete about Baz moving in with me and tails of our silly hour japes, he found all the stories hilarious and secretly wished he could spend a couple of days with us acting like the foolish boys we were.

During the film it became apparent that one of the characters, a young woman, had lead a very sheltered and religious life. She was extremely shy around men and once she eventually did marry she was less than eager to strip off naked and enjoy lustful sessions with her husband. Instead she devised a cunning plan that involved taking a white bed sheet and forming a slot in the middle where her husband could breach whilst she lay undetected beneath. This had apparently become a tradition in those times and signified a virginal passing along with various other procedures including the hanging out of the sheet for all to witness. Dear God, what on earth were we watching?

We laughed about the scene between ourselves and Baz made jokes poked at my celibate situation but I managed to brush them off with ease, I had now become used to the fact that I had something more special than any of the jokers could through at me and they backed off gradually as they knew I could turn the joke on them, well at least for my sake anyway.

The movie was great, very interesting even if it was a little bit strange in parts, Barry got his wish and the other more 'looser' girl in the film did disrobe and expose her jewels in a well presented but needless shower scene. We retired to bed and Baz performed his usual 'Goodnight David' call from his adjacent room, said in a fake Mexican accent.

The weekend had arrived and as I was attempting to save money for my oncoming visit to Mexico I decided upon staying in on a Friday night, some of the other guys joined me and we played cards and drank wine and focused on the money we had saved. That was until it became one of the biggest nights of the week and we would all in turn host the festivities and it developed into a competition of who could bring the fanciest wine, cheese and biscuits, this would then defeat the object and sometimes we would even pack up and descend upon a nightclub to finish the night. Other evenings however we would stay indoors and play that old favourite of games 'Pronounce a dessert without showing any teeth', you know the one? Sticky toffee pudding was always a challenge. Oh how the weeks rolled by.

Baz usually preferred to go out and get amongst it as we would say and on many occasions he would bring a spare pizza home for his mate, now that's what I call a friend. Other nights he would bring home a gaggle of friends home or even complete strangers, women of course who he would hold court with until the early hours. He had a new girlfriend Paula who he was getting serious with and her and some of her friends would come back and continue the party. It wasn't unusual for him to tip toe upstairs whilst I was in my bed and whisper to whoever his accomplice would be "Come and take a peak at Dave upstairs, he's celibate you know" as if I would still be asleep after the noise downstairs.

I would play along with his jokes and pretend to be fast asleep as the door opened slowly letting in the light, my covers would be up to my neck and neatly folded over as they approached sniggering then all of a sudden I would jump up and scare the shit out of them, sometime three or four of them. This would be a regular occurrence but on the occasions when Baz was alone I would get out of bed and join him downstairs for a night cap and a slice of pizza, which was nice.

One particular night I heard the drunken footsteps of my now well established lodger and his attempted quiet ascent up the staircase. He had been home for some time and I heard him fumbling around in the kitchen banging and clattering the cutlery draw, I knew he was up to something but I couldn't tell what. He eventually arrived outside my bedroom door and I could see the shadow of his feet given off by the landing light, I led still as I awaited the sound of the door handle and its squeaky mechanism but all I heard was silence. What on earth was he doing this time? Then a faint sound of rustling paper was detected and as I leant over my bed to take a look a piece of A4 white paper had indeed been slid under the door, I crept over to take a peek; he had carved a penis hole neatly in the centre, the bastard! "Goodnight David" he exclaimed.

Valentines Day had arrived and once again I made the trek to the international postal service depot which was on the other side of Manchester to collect my package from Yecora. I had also sent her a recorded package of goodies along with a bouquet of flowers direct to here office. She was so pleased to get them although sweetly embarrassed at the same time. I always looked forward to receiving packages in the post from Yecora as it meant holding something real sent from her, email and phone doesn't offer quite the same fulfilment. Inside my Valentine package were many personal items all which gave me that loving glow all the way home, along with the other items was a small teddy bear just for fun which now became my bed buddy, again just for fun, we hadn't turned soft or stupid, it was nice and we enjoyed the playfulness along the way. Barry knew I had this teddy as he saw it on my bed one night all tucked in up to his neck, I had left it there on purpose just to see his reaction, once again we cried with laughter as I prepared for the next of my night time lodger games or 'NTLG'.

I managed to get some of the group to agree to the summer holiday in Cancun and arranged all the flights to coincide with Yecora's birthday in June, it would be slightly less hot then which was an added bonus. Yecora said she had a friend who worked in a nice hotel that could offer a huge discount, which was nice. It was again all inclusive so we would benefit from the endless stock of food and drink once again. Unfortunately Baz and Kev, [Our resident Cockney, he also enjoys a good whistle and is quite partial to sporadic bursts of air guitar] had already pre-booked an Easter break to the Gambia and rather than loose their huge deposit they sensibly agreed to keep their plans unchanged. So the Mexican gang for this trip would be Jim, James, Nigel and me with Harry flying over from 'Philly' like last time, these rest of the group had other commitments but we still had a decent turnout for the trip.

I had developed a bout of serious WLF during the build up to the holiday; I had been having some serious thoughts into where my relationship with Yecora was going to lead and tried to foresee the future and what path it should take. Being the man I knew it was down to me to take charge and make decisions on how long we could maintain a long distance relationship, maybe one or two years more I thought. With that thought in mind and the knowledge we already had that we were in indescribable love, would it then finally be decision time? Should we continue like we are for another couple of years and then take a step further or should that step be taken now so to avoid any confusion and why waste two years time to do something you know in your heart is right.

I discussed this with the Fab Four and at the MNC, I knew I had found 'The one' and so had Yecora. Maybe it should then be time to act like a man and journey into a place that for me would be a once and once only commitment. I knew for sure what I wanted to do and the reassuring support from close friends clinched the deal, I was to devise the biggest secret plot since the Iraqi super gun. I wasn't going to tell Yecora and I wasn't going to tell my family, I had no idea how any of them would react, I was taking a big chance here but isn't that what life is all about?

We only have one chance in life and I was thinking big and bold was the only way forward. Forget about being cautious, forget about what could go wrong, think positive and do what feels right, all I had to do was to have Yecora say yes and the rest would take care of itself. It took a lot of balls and believe me I was packing a fair old set by this stage. Conventionally when you ask someone to marry you it would then be at least another year or two before the big day so really there was no rush or panic to fast forward to that stage, we still needed to spend more time together anyway and this could offer a more meaningful approach. When you worked out that we had only been together eight months and less than three weeks of that we had spent actually in each others company, slow but sure was my plan.

I had it all set out in my mind that it was the correct thing to do considering our circumstances, there was no time to loose and I certainly didn't want anyone to steal her from me in the interim. It was now to choose a ring, well first to find some money or just move it around like I always did. My friends agreed to keep it low key and wished me all the best, there would be much finger crossing to come.

With the holiday fast approaching and the trip already safely paid for I set out to find a nice but discreet engagement ring. I knew Yecora liked white gold and minimalist styles so all I had to do was to find a plain white gold band with the biggest diamond to match my budget. After visiting the first few Jewellers I decided to have a sit down and reflect as it knocked me sick with the prices I had been shown, Argos had now become a possibility.

I was about to give up all hope when I spotted a local Jewellers shop that handcrafted their own rings so in I walked and immediately found the exact ring I had been looking for and it was just about affordable. I knew then that again I was guided to this point and it was fate that I had found what I needed on the first day. It just so happened that I knew the guy as well and he gave me a further discount, which was nice. So now equipped with the ring in its well presented velvet box I was entering into an exciting change in my life.

Dismissing all my moaning and groaning about how unfortunate I was, I now felt on top of the world, anything was possible. I made plans to propose on Yecora's birthday and learnt the phrase in Spanish word for word, after purchasing every Spanish language book, cassette and CD available. On many a day I would travel to work and be seen mouthing "Will you marry me" in Spanish at the traffic lights.

Barry and Kev made a safe return from their holiday and it wasn't long before they also knew of my plan to get engaged, more fuel for NTLG I guess. That very same night in fact Baz had a few drinks to combat jet lag, or so he claimed and began another late night visit to my room. What would it be this time I wondered? Not the woman's underwear parade again, I hoped.

I certainly wasn't expecting the ghost like chanting on his approach, it was very faint to start with and gradually got louder the closer he got, then all of a sudden the door swung open revealing a gruesome carved African mask, I admit I shit my pants and more than a few swear words were used in my response, then we again cried laughing. This living together lark was almost too much fun to take, like being at band camp and you know what happens at band camp, well if you don't, Barry and I once witnessed a girl form close relations with a wind instrument.

So other than concentrate on the holiday and my fate that lay ahead, nothing much else was happening in our sleepy town, sorry City. The excitement of seeing Yecora combined with the great relaxing holiday we would have was all I could think about. I had a complete fresh outlook on life; I had taken control of the situation and decided I was more than ready to spend the rest of my life with this beautiful girl. My position as Yecora's boyfriend would also free me from being out clubbing trying desperately to join the many other thousands of tourists in the quest for some action. My work was done, all I had to do was be myself and have some fun, and the rest as they say would fall into place.

My last phone call to Yecora before I left was the icing on the cake, she told me of her exciting news about her work holiday rota. It meant she had two weeks free at the end of October and that she would love nothing else to come and visit England again but this time stay at my house for the duration and get to know my family a little better. This was music to my ears, if my plan worked and she accepted my proposal then everything would all be in order and above board. This boosted my confidence just at the right time and I shared this information with the guys and now they also had an added reason to believe this really was a true romance.

It would be an interesting holiday as we were assured to visit places off the beaten track and hang out with Yecora's friends some more, they were the coolest bunch of girls you could ever meet and for once we couldn't find any nicknames like we had done in the past. They were all beautiful young girls in their own right and really enjoyed having a bit of fun, not at all stuck up their own behinds like many others and very approachable. A lot like our gang in fact, they also had stayed together from school and that's quite unusual in itself. Would any of the two groups hit it off? Would there be another romance? We'd have to wait and find out.

With my suitcase packed and the ring safely in my hand luggage we set out for another Mexican experience, this would be my fifth time I had crossed the Atlantic by now and I was pig sick of it, if only it was a two or three hour flight that would be absolutely ideal. On the plus side though it was a huge relief to see the similarities between both sets of families and friends, yet another reason why I had all the belief that I was exuding.

This particular flight was not much different than the others, still very little room to settle down and sleep, endless bumping of elbows as the flight crew bounded down the aisles with piping hot drinks. I couldn't wait for the approach landing, it was my favourite part seeing the Mexican coast line and preparing to set eyes on the love of my life.

Right on time Yecora was at the airport waiting to pick us up and take us to our hotel, although it was only June it was again so hot and the car AC was a delight to behold. After much canoodling I sat up front with Yecora and the three guys nestled into the back seat. As with many young girls Yecora was rarely off her mobile phone, nattering away like they do, on this particular call she talked fast in Spanish, so fast even Nigel didn't make head nor tail of it. The call continued for some five or ten minutes as we sat politely waiting to bombard her with questions about this and that. Following a long rally of Spanish banter there was a small silence as Yecora listened to her friend reply, just enough time for Jim to shout "Chrissy Waddle" a private joke that began the holiday laughter.

Yecora was now off the phone and as we approached the hotel you could sense the whole car [excluding Yecora] was WLF about next weeks big moment, although there was this sense of worry it also made it feel special and gave us all a secret to hold onto, which was nice.

Yecora had done us proud, the hotel was amazing and it was even better than the one last year. It had more of everything and on a grander scale but we managed to pay less, the beauty of not what you know but who you know, you know. Yecora returned to work for the afternoon as we jumped in the pool and got pissed on Caribbean cocktails and soaked up the sunshine.

The plan was to keep the arrangements simple as we both knew we couldn't spend all our time together during the two weeks. Our time would be divided between a few hours in the evenings and then all of the weekend, Yecora's birthday was the second Saturday so I had bags of time to practise my Spanish. The room sharing was divided into two, Harry had also just arrived so the brothers obviously shared together whilst James, Nigel and I took the other room, already we were having a blast.

The hotel was in peek season and full of tourists mainly American and to the guys delight mainly American girls. We chatted at the pool bar to lots of groups and the mood was good, plenty of beach and water sports to do and the hotel had an enormous restaurant combining three buffet bars. You have never seen so much food in your life, mainly delicious Mexican food, we ate like Kings and drank like fish, and it was pure heaven. I had been known to enjoy my food and my top two foods were Mexican and Italian cuisines so when we found the extra Italian food court at the far end of the room I nearly cried with joy, the beer wasn't that bad either.

With the ring safely in the room safe box along with our passports and Nigel's bum bag we returned to the room for an early evening rest, this was usually the time when you are susceptible to having wild belly laughs for hardly any reason at all. As we lay watching TV and picking sand out of our arses the cocktails slowly wore off just in time to go and meet Yecora for a bite to eat with some friends.

It was great, this went on all week and I had Yecora's spare mobile phone so we could reach each other all day and make the necessary arrangements. Both groups of friends got on really well again but it was more like good friends than anything else, it didn't look like there would be any romances starting up but it mattered not, the main thing was we were all blissfully happy and with a weekend packed full of things to do we saw out the week with some clubbing in our old haunts.

Sharing with James and Nigel was great fun, they laughed at my jokes and I knew when they were vulnerable, it worked really well and the Friday was most memorable when we again spent most of the day around the beach and pool, drinking beer and feeding our faces.

At each entrance to the buffet there would be a traditional mound of bread rolls of all shapes and sizes; this must have been noted by James as later that night we were subjected to another bout of his serious sleep talking. As we lay freshly asleep Nigel and I noticed James was murmuring something so we took note and each opened an eye. We knew what was coming as it was common for James to begin quietly and end with a spectacular outburst. Suddenly James sat up bolt right and shouted "There's plenty of bread, you're a dick head" then casually laid down his head and continued his snoring. I laughed and cried myself to sleep as Nigel whimpered along with me.

During one of days leading up to the weekend I had made an arrangement with Yecora to meet her at a half way point as our hotel was at the far south end of the hotel zone. We arranged to meet for a couple of hours of 'alone time' in the early evening around eight o'clock outside a mall right in the centre of town. During the day we fooled around in the pool and again made full use of the all inclusive bar and restaurant.

Instead of having a few slow beers in preparation for my evening with Yecora we started to experiment with some other drinks on the menu, one that caught our eye was a Long Island ice tea. It sounded pretty innocuous and tasted harmless too, it wasn't until after two or three that we inspected the menu and the ingredients of the drink and found out it was a highly potent concoction of spirits cunningly disguised as nothing more than a fruit brew-ha-ha.

Two or three more and we were dancing the conga around the pool at five o'clock in the afternoon. I signalled defeat at this point as I didn't want to ruin my evening by turning up paralytic so I retreated to the room, showered and attempted to sober up. At seven thirty I was on the bus to be at the meeting point on time, the guys had decided to drink through the point of no return and make a full night of it and they disappeared into club land.

By eight thirty I was beginning to wonder if Yecora had said to meet at nine and by nine thirty I then wondered if she had said meet at ten? After a temporary glitch in form she had now reaffirmed her status as the world's latest person. I had plenty of time though to sober up and get hassle from street salesmen offering me everything from drugs to titty bars and that was mostly the taxi driver's sales pitch. Eventually Yecora arrived sorry for her lateness, I laughed it off and really didn't mind, she looked so sweet and I had been dying to see her all day, so what is a couple of hours between friends?

The following morning we rose early to pay a visit to 'Women Island' with Yecora and half a dozen of her friends and some of their boyfriends, it was a twenty minute boat ride away and sounded very exotic, it also broke the monotony of hanging around the hotel, which was nice. We all envisaged an island teeming with women but never actually found out the real reason for its name, as that wasn't the actual case. It was a beautiful unspoilt twelve mile paradise island lined with palm trees full of wildlife and beach bars, all according to the hotel brochure. Just enough time for a quick dip in the pool before we left, to my horror my big toe nail located the only loose tile in the swimming pool and split right in two down the middle. Blood poured from it as I attempted to stem the flow with the hotel first aid, this mere flesh wound wasn't going to stop me from attending the trip, and nothing was.

We meet Yecora and her friends at the harbour and she looked great in her beachwear, I however looked pale and in pain from my injury but I soldiered on regardless; a few beers and copious amounts of cigarettes would do the trick. We boarded the boat and decided to take the exciting position right at the front with just the railings to hold onto. It was great; as the boat smashed through the water it sprayed us all with fountains of sea water as we bobbed up and down across the water. Not only was it good fun but a sight to behold as Nigel clung on for grim death saturated to the bone with an expression of "When is this going to end"?

We arrived safe and sound and all took a small taxi ride to a place where we could enjoy the beach with a seafood barbeque and spend the day relaxing in good company. The taxi pulled up to the bar area and we all poured out onto the beach, now as you will know us English are not accustomed to large mutant insects and wick things. The mere sight of anything that looks like it will take your head off makes us screech like a pansy and run a mile, well it does for me anyway.

As I stood upright and helped Yecora out of the taxi it became apparent that something had attached itself to my lower leg during the ride. I almost didn't dare to look down as I felt whatever it was moving up my short trouser leg, I had to look though and be brave of course in front of my future fiancé. It was an enormous multicoloured centipede that must have been hiding on the rug in the taxi, although these insects probably don't do you any harm I jumped about seven feet in the air shouting "bloody hell" in a girly fashion. Everyone laughed but sympathised as I hadn't had the best start to the day, more reason to sink a few cold ones.

Gradually I managed to unwind and stop being on the look out for monstrous looking insects, maybe they smelt the blood that was pouring from my toe, I certainly wasn't going to swim out further than ten feet into the Caribbean ocean, who knows what might be out there fancying a bit of British beef! We had a splendid day all the same, the fresh fish barbeque was to die for and we all had a wonderful relaxing time, we couldn't have wished for more. The plan was to return back to the hotel, sleep a little have dinner, freshen up and hit the town again, once again in our large group.

We arrived back in a giddy but itchy mood after being half eaten by the early evening mosquitoes, I swear I've never seen so many in my life, there were swarms of them waiting for us as we crossed the island to the port. I sensed Nigel and James were almost ready for their evening belly laugh as we relaxed watching TV on our beds.

We had a discussion about what the news papers back home were reporting and I ceased the chance to make a small joke, to my amazement they both fell about holding their stomachs in stitches and their faces getting redder by the second. This went on for fifteen to twenty minutes, no joke, it was the biggest laughing fit I had ever seen, and when someone else laughs uncontrollably like that in front of you it becomes infectious. The three of us were pole axed but it was a unique moment never to be beaten.

The holiday was now in full swing and I spent most of the Sunday with Yecora's family having dinner and getting better acquainted. I was getting along with her three brothers really well which was a blessing because it made my life so much easier especially as I was about to ask for her hand in marriage. I devised a plan to first ask her eldest brother Hugo for his and his family's permission which is the right thing to do rather than just go ahead without consulting them first.

It would be easy enough to ask him as he was very easy to

connect with, he said things straight, as they were. He would think nothing of saying "Hey Dave, look at that piece of ass over there" right in front of his wife and mother, I think it was a shock tactic and although I wasn't comfortable blatantly ogling women in this way whilst in the company of others [once alone ogle away, was my motto], he covered his tracks by adding "You can look in the shop window, but you don't have to buy anything" as I received a slap on the back. All I had to do was find the right time to get him alone and discuss my intentions towards his little sister.

The following week flew by and we were having an exceptional time, we visited the local Mayan ruins which were nothing short of magical, we took in a Tequila distillery and visited an ecological park where you could snorkel amongst the barrier reef. Yecora had done a splendid job in the organising of our trips, all this and still carrying out her day to day work.

Whilst at the snorkelling resort we donned our costumes and slowly coasted around the rocky lagoons searching for bigger and more spectacular fish, well James, Harry and Jim did. I pretended to go along with it but had my eyes shut each time someone announced "Look at that fish, it must be nine feet long" I enjoyed it but wasn't too keen on being on the menu if any of these fishes predators arrived for a look around. Nigel too was finding it difficult with his incorrectly fitted life jacket and quarter full goggles. As we approached one of the large basins Harry said "Look over here, the fish are massive" as he lead the way. I followed cautiously, nodding and pointing with my eyes barely open. Just as we rounded the corner Nigel must have spotted something to his dislike and rose to the surface spluttering "How do you get this thing in reverse"? All in all we had a fantastic time but now all the groups WLF radars were flashing wildly at the oncoming birthday weekend.

The day of reckoning had arrived and a family barbeque had been arranged at Yecora's other uncle Oscar's house just around the corner and next door to Hugo's place. The plan of action was for Yecora's friends and us Brits to travel along the coast later in the afternoon to another resort and have a birthday celebration pub crawl in the small town of Playa del Carmen. We would go straight from the barbeque in a convoy and stay overnight in a cheap hotel and travel back the following day.

This was my chance to pop the question; I could seek Hugo's permission discreetly at the Barbeque then find a romantic moon lit setting on the beach to say "Te quieres casar conmigo"? I had said over and over in my mind and just had to deliver it on bended knee.

We arrived at the family party and I gave Yecora her birthday presents and of course a big hug and a kiss. We were the first ones to arrive at the house and as instructed I jumped into the empty swimming pool as Yecora assisted her mum and aunt with preparing the food. After a short time uncle Oscar arrived and joined me for a swim, as nobody else was around be weren't properly introduced so we made our own conversation and talked freely about this and that.

We got along great and I realised Oscar had started the party earlier in the afternoon and was already a few beers into the swing of things. Our discussion was more like between two old friends as we laughed and joked in broken English and Spanish or 'Spanglish' as it is called. Gradually more and more people began to arrive and congregated in the kitchen area, still Oscar and I were alone in the pool. Following a brief moment of silence Uncle Oscar asked "I should introduce you to my niece, who are you by the way"? I broke into heavy laughter and told him I was Yecora's boyfriend and he too laughed at the whole mix up. We had been together in his pool for around forty minutes chatting like best mates and all the while he didn't have a clue who this stranger was on his premises, funny or what?

The barbeque got under way and the birthday girl and I became the centre of attraction, we were asked all sorts of questions and made fun of, just like my family would have done. I bided my time to catch Hugo alone, the hours quickly past along with a sensational feast of food and a few beers to soak it all up. It was a great party shared with some fantastic company, but still I couldn't corner Hugo alone.

Finally I spotted Hugo leaving the garden and passing

through to his house next door, this was my one and only chance I thought and stealthily sneaked away from a conversation. As I crept in through the open front door and followed the hallway to the rooms beyond I suddenly realised Hugo was in the bathroom, this wouldn't be an ideal time to tap on the door and ask to come in, he was good fun but maybe wouldn't have appreciated being disturbed mid conference.

I returned to the party crestfallen and spotted Yecora was already packing her things for our journey and saying goodbye so I would have to resort to plan B, that would mean go ahead with the proposal and grab Hugo the following day and hopefully keep an answer of yes to ourselves until I had asked for her hand.

We set off to pick up the lads from the hotel where they were all sat in reception waiting and sinking as much free beer as they could. I asked Jim if he had got the ring and we double and triple checked before we left. Now the mood was changing and plenty of winking and hand shaking was going on making me more and more nervous.

Nigel had suddenly developed as case of sickness and diarrhoea but not to be left behind he marched on like trooper and took a more comfortable seat in the girls air conditioned car as we set off on the hour long drive. I was following the girls in Yecora's car behind with Jim, Harry and James, we laughed at the sight of Nigel suffering in silence in the car in front, wedged in with all the Latinas. Harry brought the house down with his comment on what the discussion would be like in the car in front "I bet he's whipped his knob out and asking if they'd ever seen one as clean as that" he said, we teased him for most of the journey but it eased my own worry in the meantime.

Once at the small hotel we all checked into our rooms before hitting the town, I had imagined sharing with Yecora and it would act as a safety zone in case I couldn't get her alone during the night in a more preferred romantic setting. Yecora insisted on Carolina and her boyfriend sharing with us as it would make the numbers fit all round, don't get me wrong I loved Carolina and got along great with her and Favio but I wasn't going to propose whilst they looked on, it just wouldn't work, what if I never got a chance alone with her, then the whole birthday engagement would be a flop.

I insisted that we shared a room alone, this I think made Yecora suspicious of my intentions, and maybe she thought I wanted to end my celibacy right here, tonight, what a mess. I assured her of my best intentions and told her I just wanted to spend a little quality time together as we might not have the chance again for four or more months, she finally agreed and we set off into the night. I nervously checked my buttoned down pocket every five minutes to see if the ring box was still there and I kept an eye out for a suitable romantic location. The night was brilliant, everyone got along so well, it was like two groups of best friends all together in one union, we had so much fun and it was all so natural. Yecora was having the best birthday ever, little did she know it was about to get even better, or maybe it would end disastrously.

As the hours flew by and we danced away to our favourite tunes from last year it then became increasingly apparent that there was no way I could get her alone, Plan B would be the only choice and the un-romantic bedroom would be the scene of our fate. Everyone said their goodnights and retired to bed, it was now or never.

As we sat on the bed chatting about the evening and about what a great birthday it had been I said "I have one more present for you that I wanted to give to you once we were alone". "It's a very special present and I want you to know that it is sent with all my love and devotion, but if for any reason you don't want it then you must be honest and truthful and tell me without feeling any pressure at all".

By now her face had lit up to a beaming smile and then changed to a look of apprehension. She was sitting on the bed in her pyjamas in the sweltering heat and I sported a pair of unflattering boxer shorts that struggled to contain the entire contents. I moved closer to my bag of things, took out the velvet box and moved slowly towards her, she looked on intensely. I attempted to go down on one knee but as she as so far up the opposite end of the bed it would have been a ridiculous way to propose with just my head showing so I clambered up the bed in my ill-fitting shorts and positioned myself on both knees so I was at a similar height to hers. With a flick of the box lid it revealed my budget gem stone and out came the words in perfect Spanish. The look on her face was a picture to behold and as one second slowly ticked onto two she responded with "Yes, but not yet".

Result, it was not the perfect reply but a result nonetheless. We sensibly discussed her reply and as we both had our heads screwed on we came to the decision that it was a certainty that we would marry but take our time, maybe a year, maybe two and get to know each other a lot more. This was actually perfect as it was what I had been thinking all along, we now had a real commitment but still enough time and space to develop what we had into the final article. We would have Yecora's visit to England soon enough and that would concrete the other side of our relationship, for now no dates were set and that suited us both fine. What a relief.

Yecora loved her ring, it really was nice although a little small, discreet enough to be non obtrusive. I explained about my battle in asking her brother for her hand and we agreed to keep the secret to ourselves until we had official family approval. The next morning we told everyone in our own way and I received praise all the way home from the guys, they too were relieved and could now continue with their teasing of me and my situation.

I quickly arranged a meeting with Hugo the next day and had breakfast with him in the hotel which he managed. At first he must have thought it was strange that I wanted to talk to him alone but I think he even had a tip off from his mum who in turn had been briefed about the previous night's events. There was a noticeable buzz around the place and as I sat man to man with Hugo I relayed the events to him bit by bit and described or plan and our intentions for our future. He sat open mouthed as I told him of my undying love for his little sister and how I didn't want to loose the chance of securing her hand before it was too late. He shook my hand and embraced me whilst telling me of his delight and approval at the news. He also said that he appreciated that I had come to him in this way and his father would have also given his blessing, all I should do now is also speak with his mother and everything would be set.

As I arrived at Yecora's house, Yecora, her mum and sister in law Ale were already discussing the wedding plans and the dress, they were very excited and her mum's approval went without saying. I felt an unbelievable sense of peacefulness and happy in the thought that I had done the correct thing, everything again had been a blessing from above and by following my heart and guidance an unknown influence it was simple to let it all unfold in front of me, not unlike my boxers the night before.

Hugo and the family arranged an engagement meal that evening and as I dressed accordingly in the hotel the guys were also buzzing about the result we had all wished for. I set off to the restaurant and held hands with Yecora all the way through the meal as she proudly showed off her engagement ring; it couldn't have ended any better.

Our last night together was spent with all her friends again and we were the centre of attention as we got drunk and danced away together mouthing the same words to the music of Daft Punk 'One more time', we were in a world wind of unconventional love and you could sense everyone was looking on with their own feelings of true happiness.

The bar had a facility to take digital photos that you could instantly email around the globe, what better opportunity to send news of our engagement to my family. We huddled together as a group and Yecora's new ring took pride of place in the shot, I then set about emailing the picture to my brothers and sisters. The following morning I telephoned home to tell my parents and it was my lovely mum that answered. "Are you sitting down"? I asked, she said "Well no, I was just making your dad's lunch" she replied sweetly. "Well I have some news to tell you, Yecora and I have got engaged".

My mum immediately expressed her delight at the news and she too was excited to hear the complete story from start to finish. She wished me a safe journey home and said we could discuss it when I got home, I heard her shout upstairs "Brian, it's David on the phone, he's got engaged". "David who" my dad responded in his silly manner. It sounded as if the news had gone down well with the family as news spread quickly, that was another weight off my shoulders and all I had to do now was return home and dream of the future and of what it held in store for us both.

The following morning we packed our things and prepared for once again another Atlantic crossing, this could now become an increasingly common occurrence. Yecora managed to sneak away from work to give us a lift to the airport; I was looking forward to spending what precious time we had left together alone to prolong our special moment. The guys could slope away whilst we hugged and kissed for one last hour.

This was not to be as Yecora's friend Karla, another of her best friends from school arrived at our hotel reception, I had not met her before but she had just completed her university studies and exams and was eager to get out and see people to celebrate. She was just like all Yecora's other very pretty friends but she was so excited about finishing her exams she gave off a great deal of enthusiasm. This immediately rubbed off on Nigel who to my knowledge had had a wonderful time but never managed to find the Latin romance he longed for. Even with his now well advanced Spanish tongue following lessons in England he struggled to harvest his rewards. The sight of this bubbly girl who obviously fit the bill angered him slightly and he lost his cool and ranted loudly in his posh English accent "Where the fuck have you been for two weeks"? We all laughed as Nigel wandered off muttering to himself.

We said our goodbyes to Yecora, Karla and our trusty party animal Harry of course and boarded our plane, the flight was much better this time around, maybe it was the sense of relief that I hadn't had to bring the ring home with me that made everyone relax, me more than most.

Our arrival in England was greeted with a welcome cool summer breeze as we all disbanded to our various homes knowing we would all be returning to Mexico sooner than later. First of all I had a visit with my family to attend to then an unwanted return to work to pay for all this frivolity. It would only be a few more months until I would see my new fiancé, once again in the height of the British wintertime, I simply couldn't wait.

Chapter 6

Flip Flops

I endured a full summer of missing my wonderful bride to be and much ribbing from Barry at home. We still had masses of fun living together but with increased activity regarding wedding plans it would be time to address the living situation.

As the months had flown by Yecora and I had after all the initial talk of waiting a while had in fact set a wedding date amid all the excitement, it was to be mid May the following year 2002 this meant that a lot of organising had to be done and the added difficulty of having such a long distance between us to contend with.

Barry had by now also begun to grasp life with both hands and he too was planning settling down with Paula. They talked about a September wedding the same year and another best friend George had his wedding set for October, on top of that my sister Helen was also getting married to Gary in November, not forgetting Ray and his Canadian girlfriend Nicola who he had met in Amsterdam. She was now living with him in Preston and they too were making plans for marriage. It was going to be a lively summer and autumn next year plus with the World Cup it was all set to be the best year ever.

Yecora's flight was now only weeks away and one night whilst devising a 'get rich quick' idea and inventions with Baz we discussed the reality of making a marital nest for our beloved partners. Things really had moved on since our whistling competitions, this was serious stuff. I asked Baz if he could keep his eye out on the property market and gave a target of six months to be out and in his own place by next February, we raised a glass to each other and toasted life then continued with our game of 'How many Cream eggs can you fit in your mouth at once', you know the one? We had grown tired of the

'Cream Cracker game', plus the eggs were on special offer.

I had been playing much more golf with the guys of late; I hadn't had much chance to join them over recent years as my Saturdays were filled playing football and with my long week day hours any mid week games were out of the question. I would have to be a sales rep for that to become a possibility. I enjoyed spending time with my all my friends, everybody's clocks were ticking and it was all precious time as we knew things would never be the same once we were beginning to one by one become married men.

I remember having a plan with Jim to visit Australia for the last eight or nine years to see the country and visit my brother and his ever increasing family. As we all rapidly reached and surpassed the age of thirty these ideas slowly fell by the way side and it had suddenly become decision time for many of our group.

It was a particularly cold winter by now and as Yecora could only find a flight to Glasgow airport it would be my duty to go and collect her and bring her to Preston for her trip of a lifetime in the world's most exciting City. I had booked some days off work and managed to fix it so we had two long weekends joined together. I also had various plans to visit London of course so Yecora could see Maria, plus a trip to York to see my brother Pete and his family. There were other events also to occupy our time not to mention going out with my family and friends to places in my home town, dam it, City.

I arrived at Glasgow airport bursting to see Yecora and as she didn't have a pilot's license there would be no way she could be late this time. I saw her amazing smile across the concourse and raced over to smother her with kisses. Her engagement ring was shining brightly under the airport luminaries. We had a three hour drive to catch up on the latest news which was mostly about the wedding plans but we also took time to just relax and regain that feeling of security of being together, it was really special to just be reunited and feel you were happy all over again.

We arrived at our future home via the posh route in and it

wasn't long before Ray and Nicola paid a visit. The two girls hit it off straight away; after all they both had similar stories to tell. Once Baz and Paula arrived home we all ventured out to the cinema and then onto to a pub for a celebratory drink. The girls all got on very well and quickly became good friends along with so many other of my friend's girlfriends and wives. The whole group, even the single guys who were constantly present found it so easy to get along, we had a great group of friends and revealed in the fun and parties we all had.

It wasn't much different to the way things were in Mexico although every conversation was in English, this would be something Yecora would have to get used to, I suppose as with me and my Spanish. I had made the effort to start classes but it was slow and very daunting knowing it could take years to perfect, Nigel on the other hand was doing very well with his Spanish studies and it wouldn't be long until he had it perfected in his sub conscious quest for a Latin bride.

Nick was chatting away with Yecora and the subject of my career cropped up, Yecora wanted to find out more about what I did and the things I had done. Nick mentioned my pipefitting days as a young apprentice and the only way to describe a heating engineer to a Mexican was to link it with plumbing. Poor Yecora was subjected to group laughter aimed at her as she pronounced Plumber with a B and she soon realised this would be part and parcel of learning to integrate with these Lancashire lads and lasses. Another great old friend Adam who has the most indecipherable Lancashire accent was also out one night with us and later in the evening both him and Yecora came to me in private and said that they didn't understand a single word each one was saying. Lancashire really had just met Latin America, with a bump.

We had some great meals out with all my family and I was happy that my parents and family took to Yecora straight away, how could they not, she was so enduring, lovely, sweet and innocent. It was great to see how things may look in a year's time as we had discussed where we were going to live when we were married.

Of course it is more common for the female to follow the

male and his career but of course there are cases that would work better in the opposite way, there always are. Our plans involved having a huge wedding in Mexico with as many family and friends of mine from the UK to attend then following a honeymoon somewhere to move back to Preston and set up a home and life for the meantime whilst I had a decent job and owned my own house.

Our time together went all too quickly and although the trip was again a complete success, we felt we had little time to resolve important issues regarding the wedding. It looked like we would have some frantic months ahead busily completing the final arrangements. I must admit though we did feel happier this way, with things moving fast as they did. The excitement pushed us along and rather than wait another six months or a year we were both more than ready to set sail and go for it.

We had spent a full two weeks sharing the same bed together and with the 'finishing post' for my celibacy set in stone 11/05/02 [The eighteenth was fully booked] it would mean a full two years of sitting awkwardly would finally be at an end. I had got so used to the situation so much that it no longer became an issue, more than anything it was our special way of life and we wouldn't have wanted it any other way.

We had spent vital time together and dug deeper into each others personalities and found out with more investigation that we were completely compatible in every way. Although we hadn't travelled down the lustful road of plenty we still knew that in that department everything was in full working order and more importantly there wouldn't be any gender abnormalities waiting to be surprise me. I wasn't daft, I had to have a quick peek, you hear of all these horror stories in far away shores when guys are confronting the business end of their partner only to be met with a 'Jack in box'.

With nothing but positive thoughts and lots of important arrangements made we set off for Glasgow airport and for Yecora's return flight. Yecora herself felt a huge weight disappear as she had experienced much of what life would be like when she made the huge step of changing not only her

Caribbean lifestyle but also leaving her family and friends behind. She was ready and willing and being together was more important than things that could be dealt with as both our lives moved on another stage.

Christmas and New Year came and went as we spent most of the time on the phone and email finalising wedding details. Baz and Paula had found a place and before long I was again alone in the house. It took a little while to get used to but with all that was going on I had enough things to get WLF about and occupy my mind. It was a particularly sad moment when he left because again it was an end of an era and we were growing up, we couldn't be Peter Pan and Tinkerbell forever [I was Peter by the way].

I would of course now be without the rent that Baz paid so I decided to get a loan, I had to get out of this rut that I was in before I took on board a wife who I would have to support, well at least until she found her feet and found work. The loan would ease the pressure all round and also go towards the cost of the wedding, I wasn't at all concerned with having to borrow money from the bank to spend it all in one go as my mother had always said "There's no pockets in shrouds". As with all weddings various sides of the family paid for certain things and the Latin way was for the groom to pay for the dress, the men's suits and the honeymoon. That was all fine by me and I made all the necessary plans to get things started.

I also had the job to arrange for thirty flights for the UK party whilst poor Yecora had to arrange the hotel rooms. She had more than enough on her plate already with the millions of other details she wanted for her big day. My loan would clear all credit cards, money I owed to Ann and some of the guys for my previous trips to Mexico. Also the dress, the honeymoon, my trip to Mexico for the wedding plus one last trip before the wedding to sort all the jungle of paperwork required these days to marry with a foreigner.

There was one other thing that had a special kind of feeling attached to it and that was Yecora's one way flight also had to be arranged, the only way was for me to book one extra flight for the wedding trip and only use the return ticket, it was all quite sad really that she was going to leave everything behind. The loan however would leave me just nice with my financial standing but it also appealed to me to be closer to home when I was working so Yecora always knew I was only ten minutes away from her in any case of anguish.

It was time to change job, I had had enough of commuting to Manchester and a move to Preston would free up more valuable funds. I wasn't enjoying my job as much as I had been doing and added target pressure at work with no resources to utilise meant the brick wall had been strengthened. That was it, I had made up my mind, once I had returned from Mexico in January and before the wedding in May I would also do what Yecora was doing and make a clean break, together we agreed it made far more sense.

The loan money had arrived and after securing a wonderful trip around Italy for our honeymoon and forwarding the money for the dress all that was left was to fly over for a week and log all the masses of certificates I had accrued over the last couple of months. My local Catholic Church had given me permission to marry and as I sat waiting for the letter to be signed I spotted the priest's computer screen saver which read "Life's to short to buy cheap wine" I loved that.

It was also Catholic law for me to complete a month's course in pre-marital guidance; this was particularly fun as the remaining sixteen other people on the course had a partner to interact with. In whole the course dragged on a bit, I completely understood the reasoning behind the subject matter but it was all a bit embarrassing as I sat shadowing other couples in a threesome and sharing their intimate thoughts and values, then again I wasn't all that bothered just as long I got my ticket.

There were tens of other documents that were also required to take over and submit to the high priest of the Cancun district, if one item was missing then the wedding would be called off. I had to ask my parents to write a letter to say that they had met Yecora and believe in the marriage and also that if anything should happen to me then they would be responsible for her. One of the strangest requests was for me to send a love letter that I had written to Yecora to again prove our authenticity. I'd better not send the one that mentions my humungous throbbing ball bag then I thought! The letter I did send read:

<How does the luckiest man alive begin to express his feelings towards the one he loves so dearly?

When we first met we both knew that something special was about to begin and over our first few days together I sensed a feeling of which I had never known before. Was this feeling true love? Could this girl be the one? Well before long I was certain that this girl before me was indeed the one person I wish to spend my whole life with. That is possibly one of the most important moments in anyone's life and I have comfort and joy knowing that you feel exactly the same.

So our prayers had been answered and our dreams had become reality but with over four thousand miles between us we began what has been the most difficult of times, being apart for so long. Well I have to say we did great! It is true, it has been awful at times with only the telephone & email to keep us in contact and having to bear that terrible feeling of missing the one you love so greatly that you just long to hold them and feel their touch. But we did it baby, we managed to do what so many people say is not possible. We kept our faith and not only should we feel proud of each other but we have proved we are ready to spend our lives as Man & Wife. We have shown that what we have together can overcome anything which is going to be most valuable during our married lives.

I am so looking forward to our big day; I know it is going to be magnificent in every way. We deserve to have an amazing wedding because we deserve each other, I guess it might be emotional for us all on the day but that's expected, I am sure that it is going to be memorable but most of all enjoyable. We have an exciting and new life ahead of us starting with a dream honeymoon to Italy which I'm sure will be fantastic. So then we start to live together as a married couple and I am confident we are going to have so much fun.

We always have enjoyed each other's company, I mean you just make me laugh so much, I love you more than anything from the bottom of my heart and I promise to love honour and protect you forever. We have said before that it is very important to talk to each other and always let our feelings and thoughts be known. It will be a strange experience for both of us to begin with and we have already said that we should try not to be in a position where we feel suffocated, we must allow each other sufficient time and space to have a life of our own when needed but ultimately to share our thoughts and dreams like a best friend would.

I really do admire you so much because you are taking a very big step in moving to England, I know you say that you are comfortable with it all but still it takes a lot of courage and I admire you for that. I have told you before I would like to go and live in Mexico maybe sometime in the future, also we are planning to spend Christmas with your family so don't be too scared ok, I am going to look after you so your Mother and family can rest at ease. We also can have anyone come and visit us in England and there is telephone and email to make you feel less home sick. Trust me Yecora, I will do my very best to help you settle into our new home.

Well we have only a few months left until our wedding day and as I have said before I am sure we will make each other very happy, I know that you feel the same way as me. So all that is left now for me is to see my beautiful bride walk into the church and make my life complete!>

Bloody hell eh? If that didn't pass the test then they could fucking whistle for it!

I booked yet another flight for the middle of January, this would be my seventh Atlantic crossing and you'd think that it got easier but it didn't. I booked five days off work and grew increasingly excited at the oncoming arrangements, our lives were changing rapidly and it was such a thrilling time.

When I arrived it was only ten weeks since I had seen Yecora so it was a sign that this long distance arrangement was finally coming to a close, things were now nearing what we called the inevitable. We had a wonderful week together and all the time I was dining on fabulous Mexican food, we visited tiny traditional eating establishments in the local markets and I fell in love with the various recipes and spicy salsas, it was a shame that we were going to live in Lancashire where parched peas were about as flamboyant as it got.

The week flew by as we marched on with our lists of things to do, everyone played their part in the arrangements and all the while I kept secret the full detailed plan for our honeymoon. The wedding trip would also be a two week break which would offer almost a week for us to have after the wedding to unwind and stay in hotels along the coast as a married couple, like a honeymoon warm up. The more we thought about the idea of being married filled us with supreme excitement, we couldn't hold it in any longer and itched to hitched. The bulk of what we had to do was now done and once I returned to England all the mundane things were needed to be finalised but for now we took a breather and enjoyed just watching TV in my hotel room and laughing wildly at each others pranks, soaking up the shear wonderfulness of it all.

We had just enough time to visit Gustavo who was working on the nearby beautiful island of Cozumel. We made a full day trip of it as the ferry was only just over an hour long; our only mistake was that we took the economy vessel as it was just about to leave. A mistake that led to much sea sickness all around, it was very unpleasant to say the least.

We decided that if we drank lots of tequila then the journey home would be a blur, our plan worked a treat but so also did the first class upgrade. We had a superb time and all courtesy of Gustavo, he also managed to see the funny side when we handed him his birthday present that we had brought from his mum, it was a very nice hair brush set in a fancy sheath, the trouble was he is completely bald.

I had been staying in the local Holiday Inn which Hugo had arranged through his friend. It was great because I just paid by the day in cash so there was no need to be WLF about the cost of the trip, that was until my seventh and final day when I realised I had spent all my money and because I had paid off my credit card with the loan and cut it in two I had absolutely no funds to pay. It was so embarrassing, I've never been so humiliated in my life, times had been hard but to leave the hotel without knowing who footed the bill for my last night was the last straw. I recited my resignation letter on the flight home, it was time for change and I had to get my cash flowing again.

It would be another fourteen weeks until I saw Yecora again, just enough time to get the wedding and the arrangements finished. We kissed at the airport in our favourite hidey hole and joked that we would see each other next at the altar. I flew home thinking of nothing else than our big day, this managed to distract me from the two hours of VTB that we had, the worst yet, another reason I couldn't wait for all this travelling to end. The thing was it never was going to end, once married we would take two fortnightly trips back to Mexico each year anyway to visit family so we had to get used to it.

When I arrived home I had the unenviable task of gathering money together for family and friends who were attending the wedding to pay for the flights and hotel, all separate and individually. It was the most complicated spread sheet you have ever seen. Some of the group where going for one week, some for two but I was just glad that so many people close to me were going to be there.

We had the usual complications where people couldn't make it, the most notable being all my family in Australia, it was such as shame but that's life I suppose. Then there was Ray and Nicola who where getting married in Canada, we both as couples had to agree that with everything taken into account it wasn't possible for either to attend each others big day. Barry, Paula and Nigel however did attend both, with bells on.

Paul was another; he actually paid his deposit but had to back out with work commitments at the last minute, so he lost money which I always felt responsible for. Another best friend Eric couldn't make it and he was also a great loss, he is a chap who closely shares my irreverent tendencies and would have been good fun to have around during moments of intense pressure to relieve periods of WLF. Nevertheless he wished me well in his hooey manner and hoped my findings were not akin to that of a wizard's sleeve.

Good news though that some of the guys were bringing girlfriends so at least it didn't look like I had a bunch of gay friends following me. The girls though did express their desire for the trip not to be a lad's holiday for their respective partners, they sensibly wanted a proper holiday combined with the wedding and correctly insisted on a separate hotel. Not only could they keep tabs on their boyfriends but they could also get their jugs out on the beach, result. The rest of the motley crew all to stayed together with my entire immediate family.

The time had now come at work to make a move, I had a nasty unscheduled meeting with the director who got right under my skin with his rigid narrow-mindedness so I printed and posted my CV that day from work resources. It wasn't long before I had a response from an employer in Preston who invited me for an interview. After leaving the meeting I couldn't believe my luck, the signs, the fate the guidance I had been submissive to for almost two years was again throwing me another lucky star.

What have I been waiting for all these years, the company was great, it was so refreshing, it reminded me of when I served my apprenticeship as a teenager, the similarities with each company were uncanny. I had so much fun as a trainee engineer, all down to the characters I had worked with and their unusual but brilliant stories and idiosyncrasies. The fact that I had a second interview was irrelevant, I knew from the first minute I walked into the place that it felt right, plus half of my old company worked there now also making the place feel like home.

I briefly told the directors of my Caribbean story and they very kindly offered me the job and gave me a start date of my first available date following the honeymoon. This was a complete blessing; it meant seeing out my last few weeks in Manchester, taking two weeks in Mexico, one week in Italy and staring the first full week later in my new position. Not only did I have an increased salary but I had no travel expenses as I was five minutes from home, I had a company car, mobile phone and a new exciting role that would give me my life back.

This new role would open up a whole new life to me, I

would no longer be cooped up in an office, I would be spending much more time out on the job, I would be closer to home to make Yecora feel more at ease plus I could nip to my mums for a dump and a home made sausage roll. Apart from knowing many of the people there I just knew I would be very happy indeed. This all in turn made Yecora, my parents and me all feel much more at ease. So with one last roll of the dice I made my way to Manchester before departing for pastures new, I said goodbye to dear friends I had made and caught the train home.

There was just enough time left for a stag do and as I was asking a lot of friends to pay out big for the trip to Mexico I decided on having a small evening affair in Southport. This was instead of the usual one week in golfing trip in Spain or a long weekend in Eastern Europe drinking unfeasibly strong lager whilst performing elaborate drinking games devised by Eric.

We had a much more conservative night around a few local bars and clubs with a coach organised to ferry us all home. Along the way James had arranged a slap up Mexican meal at a local restaurant he co-owned, he knew it would go down well with me and my appetite for the taste of Mexico and it was nothing short of brilliant.

It set the theme nicely for the evening and gave a chance for the guys to experiment with tequila. Again my brother Ian was absent but there was nothing much we could do about that but Pete nudged me to take a look at the bar where my dad Brian proceeded to snort Tequila up his nostrils with the highly persuasive Nick, Jim and Baz, my best men. I had decided to hand the batten to all three of them as they were equal best men to me and it kept the Fab Four nicely together. Each would perform a role befitting their talents, Baz was to do a reading at the Church [in English], Nick would hand over the rings and Jim would be master of ceremonies orchestrating the whole thing whilst Bill yet another lifetime friend accompanied them all as an usher.

With the last sparing minutes left before my next flight to Mexico we had enough time to descend upon a tailor shop in Preston where I could gather the sizes of the men in suits to email to the tailor in Cancun. There was Jim, Nick, Baz, Bill and me, Bill, we had all gone to school together from an early age and would you believe it Bill, Nick and me all lived in the same street, no more than a hundred metres apart, oh how we laughed.

I had purposely left out all the other guys from being suit wearers who included Harry, Nigel and James not to mention my dad, Pete and Rob and Gary. The reason for this was to have a small selection of best mates suffering in the intense heat dressed in a three piece suit whist my family and other mates could be more casual and enjoy an open neck shirt. This plan however backfired and could have possibly been better thought out. At the last minute my dad insisted that he wanted to be dressed as the wedding group, little did he know that it was going to be the hottest night of his entire life.

As it was such a late stage and he did obviously not want to take the cool and relaxed option I had offered for family members plus I guess he didn't want to look out of place or feel left out, so looking back I guess it was the right thing to do. The only think I neglected to think about was the group photos, my brother Pete would now be left out, it was too late now to change anything and the funny thing was Pete opted for a full suit and tie anyway ignoring my fig leaf to go dressed more casual. His wife Olwen and my niece and nephew Laura and jack couldn't wait to get there, the thought of a tropical holiday, swimming with dolphins and laughing at uncle David sweating like a pig on his wedding day couldn't come too soon.

It was going to be a long hot day and all the other guys like John, Harry, James and Nigel were going to dress smart but casual as they had been here before and had inside information. My brother in laws Rob and Gary to took my advice and they too would be in cool dress code, Gary however took this to the extreme and didn't were any underwear, well he was going to wear his kilt after all, that was absolutely ideal because it would be a huge talking point amongst our Latin counterparts.

My sisters Ann and Helen had everything under control and were a huge help in organising the group and my nephew Joseph bless him was to be a page boy, he was so excited. Another couple of friends Andrew and his wife were also coming and not forgetting the girls, there was Paula Baz's girlfriend, John's girlfriend Jane and Nick's girlfriend also had all planned their dress code accordingly.

So I was WLF that Pete may miss out now on some of the photos but it was too late to worry about such things and as with every wedding some things don't always go to plan. If you tried to have every last detail as you wanted it then you would never get the thing off the ground, how many times have you heard people complaining that they didn't have enough invites for all their friends or why didn't the band all dress the same, all these things should not spoil your day and it wasn't going to.

We had arranged for another wedding party back in England, just a get together for all those who couldn't make the wedding in Mexico to celebrate somehow with us. It was again designed on numbers and with most Catholic families I had hundreds of Aunts and Uncles, cousins and friends of the family not to mention lots and lots of friends, again the wedding curse struck whilst sending invites, a few people missed out again through no real fault of ours, just circumstance and shit happens. Eric was the most notable victim of this plus many, many dear old school friends and to this day I regret not having booked a bigger room.

Anyway the time had come to pack my case and inside next to my lucky underpants was my gold chain and nothing but positive thoughts. I had given up thinking about money worries; it was no longer a negative thought for me as it seemed to attract more problems along the way. It was off to the airport with all my family and friends for the trip of a lifetime, it did feel strange taking over the whole plane as I had become used to flying alone but it did make it go a lot quicker all the same.

I kept checking on my mum during the flight, she isn't the best flyer in the world, she is very good at concealing it however and as Gary and I queued for the bathroom for some VTB, it was Edna who was already in there; she knew the trick all along. We had had some laughs before we left home as my mum's passport was due to expire so she needed to take another photo and apply for a new ten year passport. My mum and dad went to the supermarket one day and Edna ceased the chance to use the photo booth at the entrance so she could finally get her photos developed for her passport.

These machines had moved on over the years and with many different options and backdrops now available as opposed to the press and go function of old. Brian stood chatting with an old friend after handing my mum with three pound coins for the machine. Before long my poor mum approached him and quietly asked for another three pounds, being the tight arse he is he demanded to publicly know why she had squandered her first hand out. She tried in vain to whisper "Just give me the money and I'll tell you later" again he choose to have it all out in the open and barked at her for an explanation. Edna produced a set of four freshly printed photos of her mid passport pose with Kermit the frog sitting perched on her shoulder. The three of them fell about laughing for ten minutes or more before finally selecting the correct option, poor mum is teased to this day about that incident.

My dad didn't feel too comfortable with all the family flying out on the same plane, he said that if anything should happen to us then the whole family would be wiped out off the map forever. We all said "Who do you think we are the Royal family"? Anyway Ian and his son Michael would have kept the blood line going; we all laughed it off as another one of dad's silly ideas.

We all arrived safely at our destination and the three couples were safely deposited three miles away in their secret location and you could almost hear the bikini straps fly open. We had a full week before the actual big day and set about with getting into holiday mode. Yecora was by this time still quite relaxed even though she had a mountain of organising still to do. We managed together to slowly tick off the jobs each day as we neared the moment of truth. This was good for me as I didn't want to sunbathe and have a bright red face on the wedding photos and look like a complete tourist, others however ploughed on with getting a much needed healthy glow.

Brian and Baz however must have been to the same tanning

school and both insisted on not wearing any sun block, Baz had already been victim to the Caribbean sun but still looked like some kind of traffic beacon before too long. Brian said that he had never worn sun block in his life and wasn't about to start now, someone should have warned him of the effects of the sun here as he casually bathed unprotected in the mid day sun. It wasn't long before Brain, Pete and Gary had entered into a drinking competition and as they sat shirtless with their big white beer bellies on show they soon blitzed the competition away with their fine beer swilling talents, they all received first prize, a tee shirt and a bottle of their taking. They had been at the hotel for only three short hours; this was going to be some holiday.

Yecora and I pressed on with the arrangements and it was only now that it had come to light that I had totally forgotten that Yecora's brothers all needed suits, so we quickly organised the fitting and rental of the suits, this just made me feel even worse about Pete being left out, but positive thoughts only were allowed and we marched on. I was sharing a room with Jim and I think he was more nervous than me, I had never felt so relaxed in my whole life but others around me were falling to pieces, a few nights on the town would sort that out.

Edna remarked that as long as I had shiny shoes on then everything would work out fine, "Shit, I've no shoes" I bellowed as I suddenly remembered that I'd forgotten. I hurriedly dashed out and purchased a fine pair of hand made, leather soled shoes that proved to be the most comfortable pair I've ever owned.

Luckily Yecora's brother Roman was a jeweller and we choose our rings within thirty minutes of being at his warehouse, we couldn't believe our luck and it was all a very kind wedding gift. Yecora's family worked tirelessly on the hotel arrangements which included free drink for everyone; I hoped they had worked out that the Brits can drink for King and country. There was also all the transport and logistic matters to attend to for the two hundred guests that were expected, this was to be massive party and a memorable celebration.

The two families had met briefly but a day trip was arranged to get to know each other a little better. It was Mother's day in Mexico and although the date is different to the one celebrated in the UK we still acknowledged it all the same of course. This wasn't the only celebrated day that had a different date, Christmas obviously was main one but my favourite by far was April fools day which is on December twenty eighth, it always tickled me that one.

We crossed the water to Women Island where Hugo's hotel was and we enjoyed a magical day, especially the kids who played on the beach whilst the adults had a well earned drink. This was to be my father's downfall as he had overindulged in everything he could lay his hands on, coupled with too much direct sun, he was a mess.

He had suffered small bouts of gout before in England but the sun, rich food and beer all became too much as he sat in the shade nursing his swollen foot and ankle. My mum tried in vain to look after him but he wanted to suffer in silence, not to want to ruin the trip or more importantly, the fast approaching big day. As luck would have it Yecora's uncle Pancho was a doctor and came over to lend a helping hand, he performed a quick analysis of Brian's complaint and doubled his dosage of tablets and demanded no more sun or beer, my dad was a little upset and even embarrassed that he had caused so much fuss, he needn't have worried, we all found it hilarious.

We ended the day with lovely evening meal back on shore all courtesy of a local entrepreneur friend of the family Pancho Cordoba. We all arrived at the restaurant slightly nervous as it was quite posh and formal, even the local newspaper had arrived to cover the story and take pictures.

The nerves began to jangle as we took our seats all trying to act in a way befitting the mood. Yecora and I took the head of the table as both families were seated opposite each other forming a square so there was no room for misbehaviour as you were in the direct glare of each other. The nerves became too much for Pete and Brian as the waiter asked what they wanted to drink. My dad knew he couldn't have beer, Pete knew they shouldn't be drinking beer so what could they have?

Neither of them had been in this situation before, all made worse with the waiter pressing them for an answer, I looked on with a smirk as they stupidly ordered a glass of Martini for each other. It was another one of those silly hour moments where you just can't help yourself laugh through your nose. The drinks arrived and as they sipped their drinks desperately trying not to raise a little finger they couldn't contain themselves any longer and burst out laughing. Their laughter soon turned to faces of stone as my mum's glare fixed upon them, Gustavo too had them in his sights.

Once the food arrived the rest of the evening went like a dream and everyone had a lovely time amid the classy atmosphere. Once again, very kindly the owner offered free tickets to all my family to visit his ecological park whenever they wanted; the kids were more than excited.

With only two days left to the wedding we attended a practice session at the Church, not everyone was required to be there but the ushers and best men had to come along to find out what was expected of them. It wasn't until we rounded the corner and approached the Church until Nick noticed the similarity between this Church and our local school Church back in England. It was uncanny, our Church was a unique design built in the late seventies and looked quite futuristic, this Church had exactly the same layout and structure, and it really was quite spooky, another one of those signs which had now become common place.

We quickly went through our paces but the poor priest had a severe bout of WLF, he had never performed a mass in both Spanish and English and his English was good enough but his confidence was shot at. He could teach me a thing or to about over active sweat glands I can tell you.

With a free evening ahead of us the guys decided to have another burn out and hit the nightclubs, I stayed with them for a short while then sensibly retired home early as my eye bags were beginning to resemble those of Linus from Charlie Brown.

The day of reckoning had finally arrived and I was down at

the pool side early for a swim and I met Bill and Jim, they began to tell me about the evening's escapades and Bill noticed I was chain smoking, he asked me if I was nervous and I replied "No, I just like my fags", we laughed but it was true, there wasn't a single WLF bone in my body. Just then Pete emerged from the breakfast bar so he too was put in the picture about last night's madness , I asked Pete if he had a nice breakfast, he said "Brilliant thanks, I had beef casserole, it's not about quality it's about quantity", he made me so proud to be British that boy!

I had a final chat with Yecora and she was also now feeling a lot less stressed, everything now had to happen as it was intended, there would be lots of mistakes along the way but no one would notice, only us. I blew her a kiss down the phone and said "I'll see you at the altar, don't be late", she laughed and professed she was never late, yeah right.

The wedding was arranged for six pm at the church which was approximately a one hour service then back to the hotel where we would hold a quick Civil ceremony by the beach and then into wedding suite for the party. Every body got changed and ready for the long night ahead. I had concentrated for weeks on a plan to dissuade any unnecessary worry by totally worrying about my wedding day shave.

The plan was to over worry about cutting myself badly and having to wear lots of blotted paper all over my face. The plan worked a treat, I hadn't suffered any wedding worries whatsoever up until now so I took a long hot shower [Thank God the water wasn't off] put on a brand new pare of white boxers and began a text book shave, it was all over and done with and I felt on top of the world. The guys in the room all donned their wedding suites and we joined the others downstairs for a glass of cold champagne, there was no turning back now.

I couldn't help picturing my beautiful bride walking down the aisle and the extreme feeling of it all, the enchanting mood about the place was more than special, it was electric. I was just so glad that my parents were both there to share the moment and when I saw them down in reception looking splendid I got a warm feeling inside, a feeling that I was safe, a feeling of comfort and unsurpassed excitement, I couldn't believe it. I looked around and everyone had made it into the lobby ready for the coach journey to the Church, all my family looked great, all the ladies especially. Many of my close friends where all in attendance and some of them looked terrified, I had to walk amongst them and calm their nervous thoughts.

It wasn't until Ann pointed out as we boarded the coach that dad had spent the last hour trying to shoe horn his best black shoes on but to no avail. His foot was swollen badly and he was visibly limping from the attack of gout. Ann said "Have you seen what dad is wearing on his feet"? It was then I witnessed a sight for sore eyes, he had his flip flops on!

At least someone had told him to wear black socks with them, you could only tell if you really looked closely or if he drew attention to it, like with an awkward limp or something. He was in a bad way but marched on all the same and rode the ribbing from my mates; finally Edna had her revenge for the Kermit the frog incident.

Although it was now five thirty in the early evening it was still very hot and Gary had the best idea as he wafted cool air under his kilt. I sat at the front of the coach with Jim and behind Nick, Bill and Barry. The kids were all excited and couldn't wait to see a Mexican wedding, that was until someone fouled the air with a rancid smell of fart, before I could even ask who it was I spotted Pete with the famous Swarbrick grin that gave him away immediately, his choice of breakfast was obviously now seeking retribution.

The feeling of apprehension filtered through the coach as we neared the Church, once we were in viewing distance people began to comment on the similarity between this Church and our own at home, it gave them something to occupy their minds as we spotted nearly a hundred Mexican relatives awaiting our arrival.

The first sight I had when I got off the coach was that of Yecora's mum and grandma. Yecora's grandma was a beautiful and wise old lady who always raised a smile with whoever she met and she was delighted to see me. She didn't speak any English but this often gave me a chance for some well needed practice. During one previous trip we met in the kitchen one morning and she asked me what I thought was "Did you sleep well", I responded in Spanish with "Yes, eleven hours thank you". Little did I know she had asked if I had eaten breakfast.

The rest of the group headed straight inside the Church for the much welcome air conditioning, something I bet the priest wished he could do as he stood outside soaking wet through greeting everybody. We quickly went over the various important procedures of who did what and when, by now though I was past thinking about anything procedural and as Jim said "I bet your arse is going in and out like a cat flap"?, I said "Yeah, but the priest's is taking pictures".

We waited patiently for the sight of the wedding car to arrive; this was the signal for people to pair up with the opposite sex to commence with the walk into the Church. The guys quite rightly hustled for positions because you had never seen a more beautiful group of women in your life. The bridesmaids, sister in law, cousins and friends all colour co-ordinated stood looking fine as the red faced Brits surveyed their options. Brian and uncle Pancho stood chatting about aliments while Edna and my future mother in law held hands and looked on proudly.

A meagre fifteen minutes late the shiny silver stretch limousine slowly rolled up, everyone jostled into position with me and my mum at the front and my dad and Yecora's mum behind, the wedding march began and I was glad we could now get on and begin to get married. We very slowly walked up and into the Church which suited Brian as his snail pace was the best he could muster. I turned around to catch a small glimpse of Yecora behind the long line of beauties and she looked amazingly beautiful, I felt a shiver down my spine and she also began the walk inside with her three brothers giving her away.

That was a nice moment as I'm sure her father would have approved and been more than proud of his little girl. I arrived at the altar and lovingly kissed and hugged my mum as she turned to take her pew, the procession behind filtered neatly into their seats to reveal the page boys and girls scattering rose petals in the path of the bride in her gorgeous white flowing dress. My nephew Joe and Ale's daughter Kristen walked hand in hand with beaming smiles. The first of many things not to go according to plan was that Yecora's trail had been forgotten to be unravelled but it didn't matter and it was only later in the evening when we both totted up the incidents and that it was only us that noticed these things.

The music stopped as Yecora arrived by my side [incidentally we had been positioned incorrectly on the wrong side of each other by the priest, who was now flapping like an injured bird]. We stood for a few seconds before Yecora raised her own veil as I hadn't a clue what was expected of me, none of this was in the practice session. We shared a tender kiss and held hands as the service got under way.

We managed to get through the service without any real problems to speak of and simply soaked up the occasion, even when I had to read my lines in Spanish via a microphone and loud speaker my nerves held firm only for John to shout typically "Speak up". We exchanged our vows and when the priest asked me if I would take this women's hand in marriage, Yecora replied "Yes we do" raising a wave of laughter from her friends.

Baz did brilliantly with his reading and managed to keep the sweat droplets from smudging the words. Nick remembered the rings, which was nice and Jim made sure everyone was in position for the technical side as Pete videoed the entire event. I remember hearing my mum whispering to dad "What are we signing Brian"? As they limped onto the altar for the register, it was all in Spanish of course and I laughed thinking that they could be out of house and home by the time the day was done.

The subtle differences between a British and Mexican wedding were very beautiful moments where we were joined together via a huge set of rosary beads and passed various ritual items throughout the ceremony, it was really nice to witness the ancient Mexican traditions. I noticed that the foreign visitors watched on intently.

The end of the mass was signalled by a fanfare of trumpets which in turn began a mass of handed out party bubbles being blown across our path as we made our way outside coupled with the intense sound of small bells being rung by the entire congregation. Yecora's niece Kristen had been given instructions that when the bells sound she must go and hold the wedding dress trail for the departure walk. As the trail had been forgotten on the way in it was easily forgivable that she grabbed at the priest's cassock as he attempted to make a break for it.

The noise of the bells and the sight of the bubbles was a moment I shall never forget, it was the most spine tingling moment I had ever experienced. It felt like we were being carried along the Church in a heavenly cloud and for a brief moment I did actually have an out of body experience, I've never had one before and never had one since, that is why it was so memorable.

We were now man and wife and the time had begun to have our picture taken for the next eight to ten hours, this was the worst part because although you are in sublime happiness, you're face starts to hurt after hours of being asked "This way, this way". It didn't matter, following the congratulation greeting from all the guests outside we were soon whisked away together in our amazing leather clad chariot. We made a slow journey to the hotel allowing the guests to speed past and witness our arrival, the last thing I had banked on was that the driver wanted a tip, I couldn't believe it. As if I was carrying loose change in my wedding trousers, I hurriedly found the guys who bailed me out with the drivers tip and regained my composure as we waltzed into the amazing five star hotel foyer.

Eighty seven photographs later and we arrived down at the beach front which was lit with impressive fire posts illuminating the civil registry table. We sipped champagne as we followed government procedure and had another series of photographs taken. Slowly the party of people filtered through to the wedding suite, all politely persuaded by Jim and his minions. All that was left outside was Yecora, me, Jim and the photographer, my shirt was wet through and I had had enough of having my photo taken. All I wanted to do was get inside the comfort of the salon but I snapped at Jim under the pressure and felt bad as he wandered off alone.

When we eventually did arrive it was an impressive sight, the wedding party had doubled as more and more friends had begun to arrive. The room was huge and beautifully decorated. One thing I spotted was that Hugo was having words with the head waiter, they were all dressed in sickly Hawaiian shirts and he made them race away and change into smart white shirts, which was a nice touch I thought.

I spotted Jim and gave him a wink and thumbs up to which he duly returned, thankfully everything was cool again. Yecora and I took the head table alone and enjoyed a fabulous meal and chatted about what an amazing time we were having, there were no speeches at all so that also eased any pressure on us both.

Everyone was now in full swing and enjoying the flowing booze that was being distributed swiftly, especially in the direction of the Brits tables. My dad was being kept a watchful eye on by his Doctor friend denying him beers and mum nodded to me approvingly as we stepped up for the first dance.

We had arranged for our dance to be to U2 'One', it was easy enough to perform a slow dance to and had a lot of meaning for us, the trouble was Hugo decided to play a trick on us and as we stood amid the glare of two hundred people, Mariah Carey 'Hero' began to play. We could have died, it was the long eight minute version and there's only so much awkward shifting around that we could take, it was purgatory.

Finally the music changed and the dance floor flooded with other guests enabling us to end our misery, we had to see the funny side. Nigel soon had his dancing shoes on and following two glasses of wine Edna too was bopping around like a teenager and Yecora's grandma was also throwing out some shapes, Hugo also displayed his dancing talents to everyone's enjoyment, Pete thankfully stayed seated. It was great everyone was enjoying themselves as things began to pick up pace.

The live band arrived soon after and the disco took us past the midnight hour and into the early morning. A few of the older generation decided it was time to leave; my dad ceased the chance to retire and slip off his flip flops. Everyone wished us well and disappeared into the night as the serious party animals got things under way.

A Mexican tradition of garter throwing soon took centre stage closely followed by me being carried aloft around the room as Jim and Baz took hold of a testicle each and squeezed, "Careful" I cried, "I'm going to need those later". Finally the band played our song and we danced together and gazed into each others eyes. We had had a little bit to drink but nothing excessive as we had yet to consecrate the marriage and there were things to attend to.

At approximately five o'clock in the morning we decided enough was enough and it was time to get up into that back bedroom. Even the hotel staff were trying to get cleared up and ready for a first Holy Communion party in just a few hours time. I overheard Jim telling Yecora and her best friend Luli that things would never be the same now he had lost his best mate, it was an emotional moment but Jim could shed a tear at a football game so I didn't dwell on it for long. The truth was he was right, things had changed and we were all growing up and the Australia trip was out of the window too!

Yecora and I left the room discreetly, we knew were being watched though and we knew what all the whispering would have been about. It was now our time to share the beauty of our love, well at least attempt to as we both knew this was going to be more of a formality at this late hour rather than the beautiful moment we had dreamt of.

As the lift arrived at the penthouse suite I grabbed Yecora in my arms to carry her over the threshold, her head met with the lift wall with a sickening thud, I don't think she really cared; she was tipsier than I had thought. She was perfectly in her right to be half cut; I mean you'd have to be to face this great lump.

We walked in the room and saw the amazing view of the ocean below not to mention the high standard of the room itself; it really was the perfect setting. I said romantically "Come on then, get 'em off", as I danced around the room on one leg attempting to remove my trousers. Yecora said "Can you help me un-button my dress" as she perched on a ledge. The dress really was an impressive gown and I was flabbergasted at how it was embezzled with fifty or more hand sewn buttons down the back of the girdle.

It took no less than twenty minutes for my sausage fingers to patiently undo. Once out her dress we enjoyed a romantic encounter that took us into the early morning sunshine. The waves crashed loudly on to the beach as the pelicans fished impressively for their morning feed. We had finally become a married couple and it was nothing short of wonderful.

We had breakfast delivered to our room and slowly enjoyed the romance we deserved, every second, every minute was a joy. For the next few days we had plans to stay at the hotel on the island and enjoy a peaceful break alone without any interruptions. We took the catamaran across the water and all the time we revelled in the service we had been given, it felt as though we were the most important couple in the land. Our room was the roof top honeymoon suite and it had an ocean view Jacuzzi. It didn't take long for us to get the bubbles flowing I can tell you, by now we were making up for lost time and nearby coffee tables shivered with fear. We sipped champagne in the Jacuzzi and watched the beautiful scenery as boats and ships ferried tourist along the strip of water to the resort. Another boat arrived at our hotel dock and we watched as we relaxed from our mornings exercise.

We both looked at each other with a look of disbelief as we spotted Yecora's mum and two aunts tip toe along the jetty decking, we couldn't believe our eyes, was there no escape? As it happened Yecora's mum had a two day break planned for some time and we were the ones who had booked after them. I stood up on our balcony completely naked and looked on in dismay. Later in the day the five of us spent the afternoon in the natural spa bath in the ocean, oh how we laughed. We even dined together, not directly on the same table but right behind us for most of the time. It didn't really have too much effect on us as we were pretty much oblivious to anyone else around us, so no harm done.

My family in the mean time had set off for a trip of a lifetime with the offer of a free pass to the ecological park they set off one the hour and a half bus ride. Mum and dad would much rather have spent the day in their air conditioned room, the heat, the relentless mosquitoes and the journey to contend with, but the others were really up for it especially Laura, Jack and Joe, who cared anyway it was free!

They arrived hot and bothered at the resort and they had a great time, a nice break from the monotony of the hotel, they wouldn't have changed it for the world but you could tell it had been a long day and returning to the hotel was there only wish.

We now had the situation where Yecora was to begin with packing all her worldly possessions together to move to her new life in England. I don't know about you but it usually takes longer than a few days to pack up and move ones gubbings and she threw it all into three cases full. She was going to be back in August anyway for a few weeks to complete her vital university course and to graduate and yet another Christmas trip wasn't all that far away, which was absolutely ideal. It was time to leave this tranquil paradise and utilise the spare flight ticket I had purchased, it was the moment of truth.

Chapter 7

Bella Roma

Once again I found myself at Cancun airport but this time I would be returning with my Mexican wife. Including my family there must have been around fifty people to see us off, Yecora's close family and friends obviously wanted to wave her off into her new life, a whole new world.

I managed to keep it together and thought of the fun and happy times we would have in Italy that would slowly integrate her into European culture. The majority of her friends gave their full blessing but still there were one or two who viewed the whole thing as passing fancy and that in their minds the relationship wouldn't last. Well we had to prove them wrong didn't we? We had after all spent two years almost doing exactly that by maintaining a long distance affair, why should this be any different?

The flight was a nightmare and everyone couldn't wait to get home and have a nice cup of tea. The problem was that our flights had been arranged to land in London and a three hour train journey north was there to greet us. Helen and Gary said their goodbyes as they lived less than an hour away to the south, they had had a wonderful time and they too had fallen in love with Mexico. With their wedding plans well under way they returned with a set of rings courtesy of Roman and the desire to return in six months to spend their honeymoon in the same hotel on the magical island, it really was paradise.

The next three hours were spent on the train taking in the English countryside whilst laughing at my dad opposite snoring loudly with his gob open. My mum bless her catered for Yecora's every need to make her feel better, right there you could tell that she was to become her little mate in England from hereon in. With no time to waste we arrived home and went straight to bed after carrying Yecora over the threshold once again of course, only this time it was in a three bed end terrace in Preston as opposed to the exotic surroundings we had been accustomed.

Morning arrived and we sped off in our luxury taxi to Manchester airport with a fresh case of clothing. The flight to Rome was excellent, just the right duration as any proper flight should be. On our approach we surveyed the ancient Roman City from above and we cuddled up together feeling the excitement of it all.

All of our connections and transport had been finely arranged, which was my idea and as we emerged from the airport in the late morning sunshine our chauffeur driven Mercedes was waiting for us for the short trip across the City to our hotel. Now I thought the driving was bad in Mexico but that wasn't a patch on these guys. I expected our smartly dressed driver would be a reserved character however he seemed to take out all his personal anger on the expensive tyres. He screeched around tight corners at eighty miles an hour and performed some wonderfully elaborate manoeuvres as we desperately tried to take in the fast disappearing land marks. We couldn't even get our bearings as it all whizzed past our eyes in a flash. It was at this point I discovered something new about Yecora, she had a severe problem with car sickness and she was relieved when we finally arrived at our destination.

The hotel was nothing special inside or out but if you'd seen the receipt you'd have expected a palace for that type of money. The location was all you paid for and we were slap bang in the middle of the City. We made ourselves comfortable and made time for a quick kiss and a cuddle before we set out to do a complete tour of this magical place. Believe me it was only just possible in one day to get around and see the major sights during which time we had our first argument emanating from a directional disagreement.

As with many marital arguments of this nature the male usually neglects the help from outsiders and adopts his own rational on which way is which without having to ask somebody the way. As with most outcomes in this situation the female usually proves the male incorrect and does find assistance from a simple question to a bystander. Lesson learnt.

Dead on our feet we crashed on the bed in our room, we hadn't even had time to have a sit down meal and as we were both so exhausted we decided we hadn't enough energy left to dress and go out again. Suddenly whilst having a crafty fag on the balcony that beautiful smell of freshly baked pizza filled my enlarged nostrils, as you've probably gathered I have a very healthy appetite and this was like a red rag to a bull, I had to go and see what is was missing.

We quickly agreed that I would check out the restaurant less than a minute walk away and try and get a large pizza take out to share in our room. Now this is where I learnt a very important lesson, I should have listen to my heart or even John who has always said "When it comes to eating, stick to what you know", play safe in other words. It was at this point when we should have agreed on a plain Margarita pizza or something just as safe, but no I had to go a persuade Yecora that we should have a seafood special topping, I was adventurous like that.

I wandered into the little restaurant and saw it was a lovely authentic place complete with a clay pizza oven taking pride of place in the corner. I placed my order and sipped a nice glass of house red while my saliva gently began to boil; the smell from the kitchen was intoxicating. I proudly walked back to our room careful not to open the box with my reward steaming inside, I would normally have devoured a slice or two during this point but wanting to be the cultured gent I resisted all the voices in my head saying "Go on, have a bite".

I burst into the room, placed our evening meal on the bed and flipped open the lid. We both ogled the contents of the box in complete silence. The stupid fools had ruined the pizza by throwing four huge shrimps on top still in their shells complete with head, eyes, tail, legs, the lot. It was ruined, we couldn't have stripped the shrimps without any utensils or hand towels and we didn't have the energy anyway. We picked at the ruined pizza base and gave it up as a bad job; we didn't say a word and fell asleep in an exhausted heap with the room smelling like Fleetwood docks.

The next morning and our final day in Rome was to visit the Holy City of the Vatican and all it had to offer inside. It was another full day to take in the whole place. I have always been a religious person but never over religious, it just doesn't sit well with me to have your faith completely take over your life, I was more than happy to let my faith simmer nicely in the background.

The Vatican however had a spiritual feeling to it all and we both soaked it all in as it reminded us where we had come from to be at this point in our lives. It had been a whirlwind romance but inside the spectacular Church we had a feeling of calm, we both knew we were meant to be together and so did the chap upstairs. We took in the sights of the museum the Sistine Chapel, which was breathtaking. We made time to eat this and enjoyed a real Italian sandwich outside in the main square as we watched a cunning pigeon pretending it had a wounded foot to gain sympathetic clusters of our lunch only to watch it move onto another victim and another foot.

We had a walk to the Trevi fountain and made a wish; I resisted a food based wish and opted for a more conventional thought. Just around the corner we stopped and enjoyed a glass of wine in a beautiful street cafe and toasted our new life as a married couple, there was no better feeling and our smiles gave us away as the young lovers we were.

We watched the night fall at the romantic Spanish steps and wondered what it would actually be like to be able to make a purchase in one of the many fashionable shops filling the street. We listened in on a nearby bar as it played When in Rome 'The Promise' and wallowed in our happiness. It was time to get some sleep as we contemplated our next step of our journey, we were to travel first class in a romantic train ride along the Italian coastline and down to Naples ready for our chauffeur driven trip to the Amalfi coast.

We arrived at Rome train station with our cases a little jaded and we were told to hurry as the train was about to depart. As we approached the unfeasibly long train I asked an impatient looking station master which carriage was first class, he pointed directly to the very first carriage right in front of us, what a stroke of luck and on we jumped as the whistle blew. Within seconds we knew we had been duped and not only were we stranded in economy class we also had at least twelve cramped and smoky carriages to negotiate with our cumbersome luggage. Being the gent I sent Yecora on ahead to our seats as I struggled on alone without even a hint of assistance from the sprawled out commuters, I hadn't paid a fortune for this, I was livid.

Once in the comfort of our private cabin I blew my top and called the station master every name under the sun and smashed my fist into the palm of my other hand making a loud crack. Yecora looked petrified as if I was she had suddenly discovered I was a closet serial killer. Whenever I lose my rag it usually takes only half a minute to regain my composure and this was the case again as we settled into the magnificent journey. We knew we would soon arrive at Naples as the impressive sight of Mount Vesuvius drifted on by to our left and the beautiful bay of Naples to our right; this was much more like it. As we got off the train I made a James Bond like look around the station for the fucker who double crossed me in Rome, for his sake he was nowhere to be found.

Our connecting driver was already awaiting our arrival as we headed off into the winding roads and up into the mountains ready to descend into the resort of Sorrento. Mid journey Yecora whispered that she felt a little bit queasy and I just laughed it off as nothing much, with the arrival of the fiftieth sharp bend Yecora screamed for the driver to pull over. The driver and I took in the beautiful Ariel view of the coast from our mountain top vantage point as Yecora began to throw up violently by our side, I winked at the driver as if to say "Women eh"?

Finally with stomach lining intact or not we pulled into the driveway of our luxury hotel, this was much more like it. The place was amazing and that little bit extra had given us the best honeymoon suite with the best view, I drank the free champagne as Yecora recovered gradually from her sickness, to her credit she didn't let it spoil the moment and soon recovered when we had a casual walk around the town.

The shops were much more reasonably priced and I treated her to some retail therapy and she purchased both leather and haberdashery goods, that was my idea. We had four days left to unwind and take in the splendour of this wonderful part of the world, the people were so friendly and the whole feel to the place was that of simple pleasures and all at a snails pace. Oh, and the food and wine was to die for, I could happily have stayed there forever. We even took time to go to the gorgeous Church nearby and watched as a young Italian couple made their vows, we watched on in a world of our own.

We couldn't leave for home until we had made the trip to see the famous island of Capri, the home of many famous artists. We boarded a small ferry to take us on the thirty minute ride across the bay. It just so happened that the water was a bit choppy that day and at times we clung onto each other as the vessel jostled wildly with the waves.

It was getting to the point where I was about to shout "I want to get off" as the staff issued plastic shopping bags for the tens of people who were being sick around us, the noise was horrendous. Finally the waves subsided as we coasted into the island marina. Yecora up until now had managed to keep her breakfast down but cringed when she saw the tiny bus that we had to take us up onto the tip of the island, as all the others regained their stomachs for the ride she soon had them reaching for their bags again as she lead a chorus of vomit induced sound. I politely left them all to it as I hung my head out of the window for some fresh air; I bet Frank Sinatra never had this trouble!

We did eventually enjoy the tour in the end once the group had come around. I luckily escaped any sickness but my shorts were beginning to look suspect as I imagined the boat trip back, in the dark, I had counted the life jackets on the way in and there were not enough to go around. This could be another case of 'Fuck you Jack'.

The island itself was spectacular in every way and you

couldn't help imagining all the famous people who had been here and the parties they must have had. We were told that the property on the island was worth millions, "maybe one day" we dreamed.

We eventually and begrudgingly had to say our goodbyes to Italy, at least for the time being. It had been the most perfect honeymoon you could ever imagine; even the things that didn't go quite to plan gave the situation a sense of fun along the way. We boarded our flight which was from nearby Naples direct to Manchester and all to soon we were sat in our little love nest back in Preston watching a Jackie Chan movie on my knackered old TV, maybe we could go and make our first purchase together at the weekend. It was the Queens Jubilee week and we were given two days national holiday therefore my first day in my new job would be the Wednesday and almost the weekend, I had worked the honeymoon break around these dates and it all worked out great. Now let's see what this new job was like.

Chapter 8

Lancashire Life

I left for work with a kiss from my new wife and embarked on the four minute drive to the office, within half an hour of me being at my new office I just knew it was to be the best career move I had ever made. I was given a free role that enabled me to get out and about to see the end product of each project. It was like a dream come true even though I was exhausted I knew it was almost weekend and the following week would be a fresh new start.

The majority of my first day was spent reminiscing about the same company years gone by that had given many of the staff their first working experience. We had all worked with some colourful characters and everyone had a story to tell, not a bad day at the office nattering away about the good old days and being paid for the privilege. During my lunch I called Yecora to see how she was, it made me feel much better in the knowledge that she was only minutes away in case she needed me. She had spent the morning sleeping like a log recharging her batteries and had an afternoon planned with Ann and my mum to head into the City centre for some window shopping, not a bad start to her new life, it could have been worse.

The World cup had just started and for he first few days my new colleagues and I managed to see the important games on a portable TV in the office, what a huge change this was for me, to go from intense manic pressure of the target based company of old, to this refreshing scene of happy faces and biscuits being passed around. It was superb and just what I needed at this stage of my career and life, a chance to grow, learn and surpass previous achievements but still to have some fun at the same time, I was happy here right from the word go and realised I had the potential to impress and improve what skills I had, something that encouraged me to work harder.

On of the best things I learnt in the first few days was that if I could get my boss chatting about our old firm then he would loose himself in thought and talk for an age about the things that had happened when it was fun to be on a construction site. Twenty minutes later we would quickly revert back to the importance of the job, until next time.

One of my favourite subjects was when the name Freddie Whittle was mentioned; everybody had a story to tell about this little chap of days gone by. He was a slight fellow with a flat cap and a woodbine in the corner of his mouth and I loved to hear how he caused so many people to crease over laughing with his incredible old school ways and escapades. A favourite story of mine was when he attended the company Christmas party and he arrived at the venue right outside in his van as the company directors greeted everybody in turn at the door. Freddie shook hands with them and said "This is the wife, don't laugh" leaving everybody stuck for words as his poor wife trundled inside, the man was a legend.

I liked my new boss and colleagues, we were all on the same wavelength including all the engineers and it wasn't long before I felt part of a big family and work seemed to be second on the list after enjoying life a little. Surely this was the way to conduct business, have some fun and you'll be surprised by the results.

After getting down to some serious work I found that I had fitted in quite well and I actually enjoyed getting up in the morning and heading out into the world of engineering. Yecora in the mean time had been busy with creating her new CV and set out each day on the search for a suitable job hopefully in Law as she had worked so hard to achieve her position. I tried to give her the freedom she needed to learn how things worked in the north of England and soon she began to learn more about Lancashire life.

Things were very different here in Lancashire comparing to what Yecora was used to, for starters having the disabled begging at traffic lights hadn't yet become a trend in Preston.

Or the need to tip everybody that you came in contact with even if they didn't really work to hard enough for the privilege. For me my favourite sight that I would miss was the car park attendants in Mexico.

These people had found a niche in the market for assisting people with reversing out of a parking spot even though all you had to do was what every other adult driver was more than capable of doing and that was simply manoeuvre slowly whilst turning the wheel. These so called attendants had the ingenuity and inventiveness to purchase a red rag and a whistle and hound every reversing vehicle with a wave of the rag and whistling wildly to appear that they were genuinely concerned that they didn't want you to strike another car.

Once their fine work was done and you had safely emerged from this death defying obstacle they would give the hand signal that you should cross their palm with silver, easy money eh? Some of these guys were on more money that me! They had very little overheads, just a clean white shirt and a quick visit to the red rag and whistle combo store and they were in business.

There was a slight flaw however in the fact that how would you decipher from frantic whistling and rag waving from the very same as you were about to plough into the fifty grand Mercedes behind? The times I was given the wheel I fucked up their scam by reversing into the spot which immediately pissed on their chips and they didn't want anything to do with you from that point on.

In Lancashire we also suffered from a lack of monstrous looking insects and reptilian beings waiting to scare the shit out of you. The worst you could expect was a ladybird might land on your shirt and make you jump, a little.

Yecora wouldn't see any enormous iguanas walking down the high street as she had been so accustomed. Can you believe that some people actually keep these dinosaurs as pets; some of them are as big as your leg and very ferocious looking. I once saw one tucking into a pile of dog shit one day and nearly jumped a mile.

Although things would be very different at least the most dreaded of insects would no longer be a pest, especially to me for the time being. Mosquitoes are probably the worst scourge on this planet; I wish I had ten pesos for every time my leg was permanently disfigured by one of these little devils. Not matter how much repellent, sprays or creams you apply they still manage to eat you alive and no matter how much you know you shouldn't you always respond with a flesh removing scratch. I found a handful of sand was one of the best ways to enjoy a good scrape but I still have the scars to prove it. Don't even get me started on cockroaches, any insect with a song named after it should tell you a thing or two.

There was also another sight that Yecora would be un-used to and that was construction workers obeying simple safety procedures to in order enhance their life expectancy. I had seen many times in Mexico sights that you just wouldn't believe, sheer disregard for control over basic things like access equipment or footwear.

It was common place for masons to be going about their work in open toe sandals. You could just imagine their conversations as you witnessed their morning brief on the street corner "Where's Diego today"? "Oh, he phoned in and he won't be coming in today, he mangled his other foot when a concrete block fell on him". "If you need to talk to him he'll be at the set of traffic lights downtown".

Well apart from all of this and the change in diet from healthy food to very un-healthy food the weather would be the one biggest change, if you were so lucky to have ever seen the sun and a blue sky in Lancashire you would probably be called a liar. So also gone was the sight of all the semi-clad beautiful looking people and the women only to glad to parade their 'Camel Toe', all this was traded for flat capped old men and heavy ankle women 'taking in washing', front and back.

I told Yecora that she should take at least six months to relax a bit and then slowly get to the high level of work she so longed for. In two months time she would be graduating and before that she heard news Sairel was coming to visit for a couple of weeks, she was the one responsible for our paths meeting two years previously. Maria was also coming to Preston to see what a delightful place it was. Yecora took comfort from this news and this would only be the start of many Mexican visitors to also help her settle in.

Our English wedding party night soon arrived and with her friend by her side Yecora and I enjoyed a wonderful and fitting occasion with all my family and friends to wish us all the happiness for our brand new life together. It was a sight for sore eyes watching all the Lancashire gang bopping away to Cool and the Gang 'Celebrate', but worth it all the same.

We had a great time over that particular weekend and it was the height of a wonderful summer. Each night we would enjoy watching movies on 'our' new TV and feeling like a real couple. One special moment was whilst watching MTV and seeing all the videos from the eighties and nineties when we both were growing up, we reminisced over both our stories and I always recall the song by Cock Robin 'Remember the promise you made' was playing as we burnt the midnight oil.

We both had started with a clean slate and the summer for once was filled with beautiful sunshine, life was great and we were finally partnered with the one we loved, the one who we had been guided to in La Boom by forces beyond our control.

Yecora's mum had also a visit now planned for autumn plus Ian, Anne, Victoria, Sarah and Michael were also coming all the way from Australia to spend a month with us. We had so many summer events to attend and with so many family and friends visiting it all added to the fantastic feel to life that this year had brought. We thanked God for our blessings and who knows after all these weddings coming up maybe Preston was about to have a baby boom!

to be continued….

Abbreviated Terms:

MNC – Monday Night Club

VTB – Visit the Bog/Toilet

LET – Low Embarrassment Threshold

WLF – Worried Like Fuck

NTLG – Night Time Lodger Games

GFE – Gone Fat Early

Slang Terms:

Hank Marvin – Starving

Butchers – Hook/Look

Smeeds/Grundigs – Underwear

Cockney – Londoner

Pamela and her five sisters – Palm of hand

Fag – Cigarette

Camel Toe/Taking in washing – Clothing up one's crotch

www.ingramcontent.com/pod-product-compliance
Ingram Content Group UK Ltd.
Pitfield, Milton Keynes, MK11 3LW, UK
UKHW020134250726
13967UKWH00002B/648

9 781425 168056